Live A Little

Rhonda McKnight

Rhonda McKnight

ISBN: 1508533202
ISBN-13: 978-1508533207

Also by **Rhonda McKnight**

Give A Little Love

Breaking All The Rules

Unbreak My Heart

An Inconvenient Friend

What Kind of Fool

Righteous Ways

A Woman's Revenge

Secrets and Lies

Rhonda McKnight

Table of Contents

Dedication

For Cynthia McKnight...I love you, baby sis!

Acknowledgments

"First giving honor to God who's the head of my life…" I am so grateful to you God for allowing me to tell these stories that I don't have the words to convey how blessed I feel.

There are many people's journeys with depression that inspired this story. If you recognize yourself in Raine and Gage's story, please know I am praying for you. I hope you found a little peace between the pages of this book. I wrote it for you and I did my very best to tell it in a way that honored your struggle. If you know someone who is struggling with depression or suicide, please pray for them. Prayer changes things.

Thank you to my readers for loving *Give A Little Love* so much that you inspired me to write more about the Jordan Family. You helped me to see that these people were special and they had more stories to share with the world, so now we're rolling with them. Look for more from Cree and Cade and maybe a couple more of them in the future.

I want to thank one special reader, **_Tonya Rivers_** of the Queen City for helping me with my research of Charlotte, North Carolina. Your love and passion for your home came through in all that you shared with me. You helped me put the Raine and Gage and the Jordan Family on the map, literally.

I have to thank my writing partner/sister-friend, **_Sherri Lewis_**. She is my personal cheering section in this crazy publishing world. She's also my plotting buddy, developmental editor, heart-check soul sister, and so much more. Thank you for holding me accountable, girl. I don't know what I'd do without your voice on that Vox and in my head, and in my heart.

Other writer friends, *Tia McCollors, Tiffany L. Warren* and now my sisters in Black Christian Reads (www.blackchristianreads.com), I so appreciate your love, encouragement, advice and everything else we share. A special hug to author, *Michelle Stimpson*, for not only sharing her wisdom about Indie publishing, but for reminding me that God is in control, all-the-time!

Felicia Murrell you are the best editor in the world. I'm so blessed that God opened the door for me to find you. Your gift truly makes me shine. Every word and every sentence is so much better after you touch it. Thank you for putting up with my ridiculous deadlines. I'm going to do better next time. I declare it in Jesus name. J

Finally, love to my family. My mom, *Bessie McKnight* who encourages me always, every day and in everything that I do. My daddy, Jimmy McKnight, who doesn't read my books, but loves what I do and tells me how proud he is to hold one for the entire world to see. My sons, *Aaron* and *Micah*, you inspire me to be the best mom and writer and human being that I can be. And my cousin, *Leroy Burgess*, thank you for selling my books to the readers in Columbia, SC. I appreciate you for taking the time to share my work with the people in your circle. Love you, cuz!

"But those who hope in the Lord will renew their strength. They will soar on wings like eagles; they will run and not grow weary, they will walk and not be faint."

Isaiah 40:31 (NIV)

Chapter 1

Raine Still wanted to die. Literally. She wanted her life to be over. This was a strange revelation to come to at this moment, but her monotonous life was just as it had been the past thirty-five Friday nights. Maybe if she broke her routine, stopped coming to the supermarket, picking up salmon or steak to take home and cook and eat alone, she would feel differently. Maybe if she agreed to join her coworkers at happy hour she would have had some fun and she'd feel differently. Maybe if it hadn't been so long since she'd had someone, anyone in her life that wanted to be with her, she would feel differently. But Raine didn't have anyone in her life. She didn't really like her coworkers all that much and she was already here at the store, so it was too late for maybes.

"Ms. Still, are you ready?"

Raine drew her eyes to the cashier's. As large as this city was, the cashier knew her name. Raine knew she was Amanda, because the nametag said so, but she found it sad that Amanda knew hers. Every Friday night, they met, and exchanged greetings over food and money. Habit and routine were supposed to be good, but Raine had long since believed them to be evil.

"Paper or plastic," Amanda asked. Amanda knew she wanted paper, but Raine had learned many Fridays ago that the woman was required to ask, lest her listening manager scold her for not doing so.

"Paper," Raine responded. Amanda promptly retrieved a bag and began to check her groceries. The total came quickly. Raine slid her card to pay for her items, picked up her bag and left the store. She usually made more polite conversation. After all it would be the only conversation she'd have with a human being until she began work again on Monday morning. But tonight, Raine wanted Amanda to remember that she was solemn, because if the story made the news about the young woman found dead in her Southpark residence from a suicide, Raine wanted Amanda to be able to recount the facts to her friends accurately. She wanted Amanda to say, "She seemed down or sad." Raine had no idea why that mattered, when nothing, not even breathing mattered.

She exited the store and climbed into her car. A young mother pushed a shopping cart with two small children past her door. She'd always wanted children. Raine had wanted a family, and she couldn't fathom why God had not allowed her to have the thing she wanted most. Well, second to most. What she wanted most was her parents, but they were both dead. She sighed and started the car.

The ride home was unremarkable. She entered the house, kicked off her shoes and placed her bag on the kitchen counter. Raine shed her coat and buried herself into her favorite sofa cushion. She remembered the faces of those children at the supermarket. For some reason, they were etched in her mind. The memory of them reminded her of her failure. Her failure to carve out the life she wanted for herself.

Her cell phone rang. The face of her best friend, and former college roommate, Kiara Baker appeared on the screen. Kiara had been calling for days. She was worried. But Kiara had moved to Phoenix nearly a year ago. Phoenix seemed like a million miles away. Raine let it go to voicemail like that was some kind of punishment for leaving her. Truthfully, she knew she wasn't that petty. Raine just didn't feel like talking which was unfair to Kiara, because she hadn't felt like talking all week. When the phone stopped ringing, a text message came through.

I'm worried. Please call me.

Raine's eyes became wet with tears. "I can't call you," she whispered. She tucked her feet under her bottom and leaned back against the sofa cushion. Raine was too sad to call anyone. She had tried hard not to wallow in it, but she was barely holding on. Questions swirled around in her head: *Where had she gone wrong? How did she let herself come to this place?*

She went to college, started a career like every other woman, but then she stalled. Nothing happened. She'd had no series of boyfriends or dates that would get her closer to marriage. Was she so utterly unapproachable that she'd warded off every man that would have thought she was halfway decent looking? Or had the years of teleworking in isolation and the evenings and weekends spent working at Hope House with the homeless cut her off from civilization? Raine didn't know if it was her or her lifestyle that had brought her to this place. But she did know she was tired of it. She was tired of the life she had. Living it everyday had become a burden and she had no idea how to change it.

Raine stood and left the living room for the office/sitting room. She'd converted her formal dining room into this tranquil space. It was her favorite room in the house. She'd had a window seat installed under the bay window and covered the seating with a brocade floral fabric in a satin finish that had just the right shades of rose and mint green. Next to the window was her writing table, an antique Queen Anne style desk that she and her mother won at an auction. This little nook was where Raine read, relaxed, dreamed, and where she penned those dreams in her journal.

On the wall above the desk she had a sign her father had carved and painted for her that read, *A Room of Raine's Own.* The phrase was taken from the title of an essay she'd read in college by Virginia Woolf. Raine had talked about the insight of Ms. Woolf endlessly the summer she'd read the essay.

13

Eight years later when she purchased her house, her father surprised her with the sign. He'd remembered her rambling and his effort blessed her so. Raine didn't think there was anything more valuable in her entire house than that gift. She smiled just thinking about the joy it had given her over the years.

She looked to the right. On the other end of the room was her home office. She'd been teleworking three to four days out of the week for a few years. That space had the same relaxing themes, but it was in sharp contrast to her woman cave in terms of relaxation. Though it paid extremely well, Raine despised her job and the only reason the two spaces were in the same room was because her company required teleworker's home offices to be on the first floor of their dwelling. No stairs reduced the company's liability for worker's compensation related injuries at home. Since this was the only room on the first level of the house besides the kitchen, living room and a powder room, this was it. She'd planned to move her private little nook, but then her dad had passed away and her mother became ill shortly after. Now she had no desire to move it. Besides, she was able to compartmentalize the spaces and ignore one when she was in the other.

Raine took a seat at her writing desk, opened the door and removed a prescription bottle of pills that she had placed there. Two months of sleeping pills. Sixty pills would put a dinosaur in a comma. They would surely end her misery. She opened the bottle and poured the pills out. She played with them for a few minutes, taking in the smooth, hard texture. She lined them up in rows of ten like white lines of cocaine across the width of the forest green desk blotter.

Were these tiny little pills the answer to all her problems? Could she really just take them and disappear into heaven with her parents? Disappear from the hell she was living that was void of anyone. She was convinced they were.

Hanging herself seemed gruesome. Raine had already failed miserably at slitting her wrist. She didn't like pain. Escaping pain was the whole point. She sighed. Her stomach growled like a hungry bear was inside of her. She hadn't eaten since morning. Taking pills on an empty stomach might cause her to vomit and that would be disastrous. She'd read stories about people who failed at overdosing on pills turning into vegetables. That was not going to be her story. She was going to be successful this time. God himself was going to have to come down from heaven to stop her. Raine was determined when she closed her eyes tonight she would wake up on the other side of life. She stood and went to the kitchen to make her last supper.

***

Raine stared at the phone until it stopped ringing. It had been a local number. She didn't know anyone local that would be calling her after nine on a Friday evening, so she decided it was a wrong number. She ignored it and went back to writing the letter she was leaving for Kiara. Raine looked at the glass of water and the pills. It wouldn't be long before she'd be done with her short note and then she'd have to take the next step, swallowing them all. She felt overwhelmed by the thought. Her throat closed. She could hardly breathe enough to push the words out of her mind and onto the paper.

The phone rang again. *Answer it*, a voice in her head said. So instead of ignoring it again, she swiped the screen.

"Hello, may I speak to Raine Still?"

"This is she." Raine rolled her eyes. Who else would it be? It was her number.

"Oh, Raine, thank goodness. This is Elissa Wilson from

the arts council. How are you, dear?"

She immediately regretted her snarky thoughts. Her mother had loved this woman. "I'm well." Raine put down the pen and pushed the sheet of paper away from her.

"That's good to hear. Well, I do apologize for calling at the last minute, but we have tickets for you."

Raine frowned. "Tickets?"

"You called a few months ago about tickets to The Show. At the time we were sold out. I know how much your mother, God rest her soul, loved The Show and supported it every year. I felt horrible that we were sold out."

Raine closed her eyes and opened them to possibility. "Ms. Wilson, are you calling to say there are tickets?"

"Why yes, dear. I didn't know that our director put tickets aside in your mother's name. I just discovered this a week ago, but I didn't have a contact number for you. I sent a few emails but you didn't respond. It occurred to me that the secretary at Oak Hill Church would have your phone number, so I called her up and begged for the number. Again, I apologize for the late notice. She just got back to me less than ten minutes ago."

Tickets to The Show. Raine closed her eyes to the delight of it. Her mother's very favorite thing. She had promised her mother she'd continue to support the arts council. She'd done so with monthly donations from her bank account, but she'd missed the deadline to get tickets for this year's performance.

"You must support and attend the theatre. The arts are important. Culture is important. The only thing that separates us from the animals is culture and education." She'd heard that countless times during her childhood and on up into her adulthood.

"I won't see my grandchildren, but make sure you take them to the theatre. Introduce them to museums and the ballet. Make sure they see

The Show every year."

Raine felt lightheaded. She was glad she was sitting or she surely would have fainted and hit the floor. "Tell me, Ms. Wilson, when can I pick up the tickets?"

"Well, that's just it, dear. Like I said, it's last minute. Our fault here. Please understand."

She was getting frustrated with the drama, but she kept her tone even and courteous. "It's fine, Ms. Wilson. Please give me the details."

"The tickets are for tomorrow night's performance. Nine p.m. They'll be at the window in your name."

Raine nodded. Tomorrow night was perfect.

"There are four of them," Ms. Wilson said interrupting her thoughts.

Raine frowned again. "I only need one."

"Well, you have four. Perhaps you can invite friends to join you. There's no charge for them, so you never know, people may be willing to shuffle plans around for free theatre tickets."

Friends. Raine almost laughed out loud. She didn't have any of those. "I doubt that'll happen, Ms. Wilson. I think it would be better if you tried to sell them or gift them to someone else."

"It's too late for that. If you can't use them, they'll just go to waste. Please do try to find a taker amongst your friends."

Raine nodded. "Of course. I'll see what I can do. Thank you, Ms. Wilson. Thank you so much for tracking me down."

"Enjoy the performance, dear."

They ended the call.

Raine looked at the pills and the paper and pen. She raised her hands to her ears, covered them and shook her head.

"What am I doing?" Her voice was a desperate squeal. She was shamed. Her parents wouldn't want her to do this. Even though she wanted to see them again, they would not want to see her. Not dead at thirty-four. Her mother had to reach down from heaven and put tickets in front of her to make her see that. She groaned. The anguish from her pain filled the quiet room. Raine dropped her arms, turned her wrist up and looked at the scars from the time she'd cut her wrist a year ago in an unsuccessful attempt to end things after her mother's funeral. Why had she let the idea of death consume her? Why couldn't she find the will to fight for her life? She didn't know, but she did know one thing. She was not killing herself tonight. She had a date with her mother tomorrow.

Raine stood, left the room as it was and went up the stairs to her bedroom. She opened the closet and walked to the rear where she kept dresses for formal occasions. She chose one she'd purchased but had never worn. It was perfect for a night at the theatre. She hung it on the hook inside her closet door. Walked to her bed, climbed in and pulled the comforter over her body. Her mother's show. Raine had a reason to live another day. God had given her the sign she prayed for. Maybe there was something she was supposed to do with her life after all.

Chapter 2

Gage Jordan wasn't crazy about the theatre. In fact, at this stage of his life, he wasn't crazy about anything that was pretend. Having received his medical discharge papers after serving his fifth tour in the Middle East, he wasn't able to reconcile anything pretentious or frivolous with the reality of life in the war torn country he had called home for more of his adult years than the country he actually called his real home. But it was his parent's anniversary. They wanted their children in attendance and standing at attention he would be.

His cell phone vibrated. He removed it from his pocket. The installed walkie-talkie app had an incoming message. He pushed the button and listened.

"You are as slow as an old woman, Gagey. Forward march your hind parts down the stairs."

A smile touched his lips. His sister, Cree was as animated and descriptive as she had been the day she uttered her first word, which was not mama or daddy, but paday which was her version of party. And she was right. They had been waiting for him for much too long.

He stood and took the two steps that closed the distance between the tub and the sink. Gage had been dressed for more than twenty minutes. Instead of exiting his bedroom and making the trip downstairs to join his family, he'd been hiding out in his bathroom. He'd been hiding from rest of the evening, because he'd already given just about all the mental energy he had to his family.

It had been a long day. It began with breakfast with his

parents, served by his older brother, Chase, a gourmet chef with a rising star of a catering business. During breakfast, anniversary gifts were presented and love and laughter were exchanged, as they took a long trip down memory lane. Then the Jordans met for an early dinner at his parent's new favorite restaurant, The Cajun Queen, where they had ridiculous cuts of blackened steak and enormous prawns covered in rich and decadent Creole sauces.

Then, as if that wasn't enough, they piled into their cars and met up at The Crave Dessert Bar, one of Cree's haunts. There everyone loaded up on cheesecake, pies, cupcakes and every other manner of high caloric, sinful dessert they could shove in their mouths. And now they were headed to the theatre for their annual get together to see The Show.

The Show was a variety presentation of various local talents, many of them children. Most of it was musical and included singing, dancing, and instrumental performance pieces. There was even some comedy. It was family friendly, entertaining, well done and any other positive words Gage could think to describe a show of its kind, but singing and dancing and humor were hardly palpable for him. Not at this time.

"You're a soldier," he whispered to himself as he raised his hand to straighten his tie knot. In some ways, his battle to re-enter civilian life was worse than the war had been overseas, but he was making the transition, one day at a time.

Gage exited the bathroom, his bedroom and took the steps as quickly as he could. Clapping loudly as he entered the room he shouted, "Okay, let's go show them that we can show up on time for The Show."

Cree stood and closed the distance between them. "You look handsome. I think this is the first time in years that I've seen you in a suit that wasn't issued by the Army." She pursed her lips. Then frowned as she studied his tie. "Didn't Uncle Sam teach you how to center your tie?" She reached for the knot. Gage grabbed her hands a little more forcefully than he intended to.

"It's as straight as it needs to be," he said apologizing with his eyes after he released her.

Cree's bottom lip quivered. She whispered, "Are you okay?"

He nodded. "It's been a long day and I've only been home a few weeks. I'm adjusting."

Cree frowned again and sighed in much the same manner as she had the other times he'd reminded her that he was adjusting. He knew she didn't mean any harm. She just wanted her older brother back and having no frame of reference for all that he'd been through meant she had high expectations for that to happen. Gage knew it was impossible. He'd been changed forever by the war. But he could pretend with the best of them, so he forced a grin, clapped his hands again and barked the order, "Line up Jordan Clan."

His siblings stood and lined up at the door in order of birth. Doing so was a habit they'd carried over from childhood. Their mother, Evelyn Jordan, said it was easier to keep up with them if they stood in line in ascending order of the way she'd birthed them, so it began with the youngest, Arielle, followed by Drake, Cree, Cade, Brooke, a space for him and then finally, the oldest of the group, his brother, Chase. The only difference in the line up now was that all three of his brother had wives next to them, but they were still the Jordan seven.

They exited Brooke's townhouse, and filled as few vehicles as they could get into comfortably. Their parents, driven by a limo they'd rented for the occasion, were probably already in route to the theatre.

Brooke, Cree, and Arielle happily climbed into his Hummer. The truck was a gift Gage had purchased for himself with the intention of celebrating his exit from the military. He now realized that not only had it been a spontaneous overindulgence, the vehicle also symbolized a military tank. He'd only managed to remind himself that his permanent disability retirement from the Army was not a thing he wanted to celebrate.

He said a prayer of protection as he always did before he started an engine and then Arielle turned on the radio and filled the car's cabin with music that she and Cree rocked and sang to. He and his sister Brooke, the old folks at thirty-six and thirty-four respectively, admonished them to lower the volume on their vocal collaboration. They did so, but only for a minute.

Gage trailed behind the other two cars. Chase and his wife, Pamela and Drake and his wife, Olivia were in one vehicle and his brother, Cade and his wife, Savant were in another. Cade and Savant never joined anyone no matter how much room was in the car. It was said that Savant was not easy to share a small space with. Gage had been gone for fourteen years so he didn't know. But he assumed it was true, because his brother, once fun and lively, seemed stressed and burdened. The man's chest was less out than it should have been. He was graying early, which was something Jordan men didn't do. Gage knew better than anyone what stress could do to a man. His career in the military had taught him that stress killed if it was not properly managed. Even if one took the time to exercise, eat right, and get proper rest, they still had to take control of their mind or thoughts about the things that were stressing them would eat them alive. That he knew for sure, because his own mind had practically devoured him whole.

The three car caravan moved effortlessly through the streets of Charlotte, from Myers Park area where most of his siblings lived to the Plaza-Midwood area where the East Charlotte Black Art Theatre was located. When they arrived, their parents, Nathaniel and Evelyn Jordan were stepping out of their limousine.

Gage observed his father's tender handling of his mother. Of all the men he'd respected in his fourteen year career in the military, he had never met a man that he thought more of than his father. Forty years of marriage and an unquestionable devotion to a woman he met and married in a week, seven children and a successful business in Jordan Home Renovations that they had grown together and were now transitioning to sons Cade and Drake was a lot to admire. He didn't know many people who could testify to such a fine example of commitment and hard work.

He followed the other two cars into the parking lot outside the small theater, hopped out and opened the three passenger doors and helped his sisters down from the tall vehicle.

"That was a nice ride," Arielle crooned. "As soon as I get good and in the black I'm going to get me a nice used H2." Arielle had just started a business management consulting company. She was working hard. But business was contract to contract with some weeks in between clients, which made her anxious. Her father and siblings assured her that all entrepreneurs had to build a portfolio and that a business didn't grow overnight. Gage was proud of her for leaving corporate America and doing her own thing.

"You can take this one off my hands if I don't get a job soon," he replied.

Cree laughed as he reached in to help her. "You're going to get that job with the feds next week." She reached up for his tie and pushed the knot again. "What's wrong with this tie?" This time he didn't stop her from her manipulation. "I'm not used to you not being all buttoned up properly."

A smile lifted the corner of his mouth. "Maybe I'm trying to relax my look. Who knows, next week I might show up with a blazer and no shirt."

All three of his sisters laughed.

It was Brooke who said something this time. "It doesn't hurt to do something different. Especially if what you've been doing isn't working."

Cree smirked. "Listen to Ms. All In Love trying to tell someone to step out of the box. If it wasn't for me, you'd still be tied to some laptop doing that work-a-holic thing."

Brooke planted her hands on her hips. "Do not try to take credit for the new me. My man helped me to step away from the computer. Not you."

Cree rolled her eyes. "Yeah, but I had to convince you to give your *man* a chance. You almost blew that."

Brooke waved Cree's statement off. "Ain't nobody got time for all this fiction. Mom and Dad are waiting for us."

They met up with their coupled siblings and made their way across the street to the theater.

The smile on his mother's face made the effort to be here worth it. She'd supported this venue since the days when she and his father lived in the neighborhood and that had been more than twenty years ago. The effort began with an afterschool program in a small community center. Drama, music, and visual arts were introduced to low income children in the neighborhood. Soon it became apparent that the children loved acting and dancing and singing more than anything else, so the center director shifted most of the activities that way and The Show evolved. The Black History Show known simply as The Show was a showcase of different scenes from slavery to the civil rights movement. Adults were also in the performance and every year they managed to get a celebrity to join the cast. This year the spotlight would be on television and movie personality, Loretta Divine.

Cree and Brooke joined their mother in the line to pick

up tickets and the rest of the group waited off to the side and debated about whether or not the Panthers would go all the way in the playoffs.

"What do you mean? I spoke with Ms. Wilson yesterday." Gage heard his mother say. There seemed to be some kind of misunderstanding at the box office that his brothers and father had not yet become aware of because of their banter about football. Gage left the discussion to see about the issue his mother was having.

"What's up?" he asked.

"There's a mix up with the tickets. They're trying to work it out now." Cree's mouth was a thin line of disappointment. "I don't know why these people won't email you tickets. All this 'will-call' at the box office is prehistoric."

"Or at least pre-email," Gage teased.

Cree hit him playfully and more light entered her eyes. "You got jokes. It's good to hear one come out of your mouth."

He swallowed a protest. It was true that he'd been less than fun to be around since his discharge, but he was trying. He was trying so very hard and no one in world understood all that he was dealing with. They had no idea how hard it was to transition to civilian life after being a soldier for nearly fourteen years. And then there was his guilt over what had happened to his friend, J.J., during his last assignment. Gage was still trying to recover from that. Before his mind wandered back to the memories, he heard Brooke exclaim loudly.

"Oh my goodness! Raine Still!"

Gage and Cree turned in the direction of the woman who had caught Brooke's attention. Brooke closed the distance between Raine and herself. It seemed to take a few seconds for her to recognize Brooke. When she did, a warm smiled formed over brilliant teeth. She accepted the heartfelt hug from Brooke. Before they parted, Raine looked over Brooke's shoulder right into his eyes. Gage felt his stomach drop.

"How are you?" Brooke asked, pulling Raine's attention back to herself. They began the girl chatter involved in catching up.

Gage couldn't pull his eyes away. Her elegant shoulders rose and fell as she released an exaggerated huff about her dress being an old thing when Brooke complimented it. She raised a hand with long, pretty fingers to sweep her shoulder-length, straight styled hair behind an ear.

Cree's voice sliced through his thoughts. "Wasn't she in school the same time you were?" Then she waved off her question. "Never mind. You probably wouldn't remember her. She was a few years behind you."

I remember her, he thought. It had been years since he'd seen her. "She attended Cade's wedding," he offered like that was his only instance of acquaintance. It was not.

Cree frowned. "That's right. Her mother sang."

Gage's exchange with Raine at the wedding had been brief. A dance that he'd wished could have lasted longer. But her mother became ill, something about eating nuts and needing to go home to take Benadryl. The sudden break seemed just as disappointing for her as it had been for him. Two days later he'd shipped off for his first tour to Afghanistan. That had been his first of two encounters with Raine.

"You all remember Raine," Brooke said as she practically pulled the woman by her arm toward them.

"Of course," Cree replied as she stepped and air kissed her. "It's been a minute. Fab dress."

She thanked Cree and then raised her eyes to his again.

26

Gage thought his heart would come out of his chest. She hadn't changed. He knew that because he remembered every line of her beautiful face, which seemed to have gotten better looking over the years, probably because she'd filled out some. She was a skinny teenager. Scrawny might be an even a better description. Braces and a mass of wild curly hair that no ponytail holder or cornrows seemed to tame, at least not by her adoptive Caucasian mother. But she was pretty. He remembered always thinking those huge brown eyes would make some man melt one day.

Gage had been a senior when she entered their high school. Captain of the football team, he'd been tied down with the head cheerleader. But he'd always been curious about Raine Still, the loner with the eccentric seventy year-old parents. That's why he'd asked her to dance that night at the wedding. That's why his heart was pounding out of his chest now.

Gage spoke her name as a greeting. "Raine." He didn't know if he was supposed to hug her or shake her hand, so he did neither. She smiled coyly, but those big brown eyes were not shy. "It's good to see you again," he added.

Before she could respond, their mother broke the conversation. Her face was a mask of disappointment. "You're not going to believe this."

"What is it?" Cree asked.

"They don't have all my tickets." His mother practically cried out the words. She handed the tickets to Cree and reached into her handbag for a tissue.

"Well, are they sold out?" Brooke asked.

"You know this show sells out before Halloween every year." His mother continued. "This is ridiculous."

They were regrouping and trying to figure out what they could do when Raine spoke up.

"Maybe I can help." Her words offered hope. She was speaking to his mother, but she drew her eyes to his for a moment. "How many do you need?"

A curious expression came over his mother's face and while frustration still tainted her words, there was a slight lilt in her tone when she replied, "Just two."

"I have two extra tickets," Raine said and then she smiled. It was a smile that was brighter than any of the stars in the sky. Gage felt his stomach drop again.

Raine swept past Cree and went to the now empty ticket counter, exchanged a few words with the gentleman there and came back with two tickets in her hand. "I had four, but I don't need them."

His mother blinked, then broke into a gracious smile. "Are you sure dear?"

Raine nodded. "Of course I am."

"What do we owe you?" Gage interjected removing his wallet from his pocket. He knew from the conversation in the car ride that the tickets were expensive.

Raine shook her head. "Oh, no, they were complimentary, so…" Her eyes met his again and her voice came across with a nervous tremble. "They were free."

Gage returned his wallet to his pocket. She was blushing. *Still shy*, he thought. And he still found it incredibly sexy.

Brooke's interruption broke their gazes. "You're a godsend, Raine. Mother, you remember Raine, her mother Amanda Still sang at –"

Evelyn Jordan gave Brooke a look that shut her eldest daughter's mouth. "Of course. Her mother and I worked on the arts council together for years. How could I not know her?" She leaned in and gave Raine a motherly hug. "How have you been, honey?"

Raine closed her eyes, and made the hug deeper as she held on longer than most would with someone who wasn't family. If Gage didn't know any better he'd think she was soaking in some motherly love. When the hug broke, Raine replied, "I've been fine, ma'am."

His mother continued, "I tried to reach out to you after the funeral."

Raine nodded. Her eyes became misty and her voice trembled some more. "I know, Mrs. Jordan. I apologize for not responding."

His mother nodded understanding. "I know it's been hard."

"Yes, ma'am," Raine was gracious, but Gage knew she was heartbroken. He could see it in her eyes and hear it in her voice. He wondered who had passed away. Both her parents had to be in their late eighties.

"Are we going in or not?" Savant Jordan, Cade's irritable wife, interrupted in a less than amiable tone. "I'd love to take these five inches off underneath my feet. It's cold out here and it's going to get crowded in there. We don't want to have to sit in the back."

The air in their space suddenly got a little chillier. Cree handed her all but four of the tickets. Through a tight smile she said, "Why don't you disperse those, Sugar, and go on in."

Gage noticed everybody's smile was tight around Savant. The failing actress seemed to be failing at more than her career. Gage also noticed she and Cade were at each other's throats most of the time in arguments sparked by her temper. Rumors of a separation were in the air. Jordan's didn't end marriages, so Cade was holding on for dear life.

Savant swished away. She shoved all of the tickets but two at Arielle, took Cade by the arm and pulled him into the theater with her. Gage wondered if it was normal for her to run down a list of complaints like she'd just done. Shoes, cold, crowd...he felt sorry for his brother.

The rest of the family stepped to their party. After introducing Raine as an old friend, Brooke announced it was time to be seated because a swarm of people were coming from the parking lot.

His parents locked arms. His father said, "I should make y'all line up."

The Jordans laughed and their little crowd made a move to the main entrance.

Brooke hung on to Raine for a moment, expressing how good it was to see her, but then looked around and asked, "Who are you here with?"

Raine's bottom lip quivered and the glow left her eyes. She shrugged. "Late. I'm sure they'll be here in a minute."

Gage sensed her disappointment. True to herself, Brooke offered, "Come in and sit with us until."

Raine declined with a shake of her head. "I might have missed seeing their car go into the parking lot while we talked. Really, it was wonderful seeing you again, Brooke. You look fantastic."

Brooke smiled widely. "So do you."

Gage couldn't agree more. Brooke looped her arm through his and said, "Thank you so much for the save. It's our parent's anniversary, so it's a special night."

Raine tilted her head to the left and said, "Please congratulate your parents for me. It was my pleasure to help with the tickets."

But something about those tickets hadn't been her pleasure. Gage could see it in her eyes. They weren't quite as bright and the smile on her face reminded him of the one

Cree had given Savant. It was disingenuous, but in a sad way.

"Good to see you again." He nodded and fell into step with his sister.

Gage released Brooke's arm to allow her to enter the single door ahead of him, then glanced back. Raine was not facing their direction. He hesitated, hoping she would, but she continued to look towards the parking lot.

Her date is late, he thought. Must be a woman because surely a man would have picked her up at home. He chastised himself for wondering if it was some out of order dude. That was none of his business, but the rapid beating of his heart made him think he wished it was. He pushed the thought from his mind before he slipped through the door to join his family.

Chapter 3

While everyone else in the theater was laughing and applauding the hilarious antics of the comedic scene the children were doing around the early civil rights era, Raine was clutching a wad of tissues and fighting to keep racking sobs inside. She was glad the theater was pitch black. She was also glad she'd been the last person to be seated. It allowed her to take the seating that was leftover, one of two in the very rear of the venue.

Although she was sad to be attending The Show without her mother for the first time in the twenty years since its inception, Raine was more saddened by the fact that she had nearly missed it. She'd not taken the time to reserve her tickets the way she knew she needed to, because she couldn't bear to talk to anyone that was going to offer her condolences. There was no consoling her. Her heart was broken into two pieces in her chest. She had no idea how it managed to beat.

A raucous round of laughter came from the audience for the comedic line Loretta Devine had just delivered. Raine smiled. Getting Ms. Devine was impressive. The older crowd in the audience was sure to enjoy her performance more than they had that kid from that nineties sitcom the arts council had invited last year. Raine couldn't even remember her name, but she did remember her mother's thoughts about it. "I don't know who hired that little, no talented child." Raine smiled. There was little room for compromise in any area of the Still family's life, but The Show was never to be second rate.

She released a long sigh. Instead of pitifully wallowing in her own sadness, Raine focused on the performances. The kids were so good. Her mother would have been proud of them this evening. She was glad she'd pulled herself together, because they were even better this year than they had been the last.

Little Shaneka Borden, the mean neighborhood girl, had lost weight and grown so much that she almost looked willowy. Todd Walker, the son of a recently imprisoned man who was formerly one of the biggest drug dealers in Charlotte, had learned to listen. He was singing in the chorus and had two lines as a runaway slave on the Underground Railroad sequence. All the kids were fantastic. Not one of them missed a step or forgot a line.

Oh God, Raine cried out in her spirit. *The work had not been in vain.* Her mother's work had always produced something of value. More tears erupted from her soul. Why wasn't she more like her?

She stood. It was near the end. She needed to leave before anyone saw her. There was no hiding her red rimmed eyes and running nose. She hated sympathy and pity. She hated the empty words that came with them, so like Cinderella escaping the ball Raine rushed out of the main seating area and made her way to the restroom. After she patted her eyes with some water and put in a few eye drops, she blew her nose one more time and exited. She could hear the applause and knew the finale was coming soon. Glad she'd escaped in time, she rushed across the street to the parking area as fast as her metal stilettos would carry her.

Seeing as how she was one of the first people to arrive this evening, her car was at the front of the lot. She passed a large black Hummer with an Army bumper sticker. The license plate read Gage J. It was a sexy car. *Just like him,* she thought. Gage Jordan. Nothing about him had changed except for the better. His dark eyes, smooth skin, deliciously long dimples, perfect teeth, and impressively broad shoulders were just as she remembered.

Brooke had not known it, but she'd been expecting them. As the man at the ticket booth moved down the list of ticketholders she'd seen the name Evelyn Jordan and a party of ten, which she now knew should have been twelve. She had no idea if Gage would be with them. She actually suspected he probably wouldn't, but she couldn't help hoping he was. Raine knew he was in Charlotte. She'd read it in the local newspaper. He'd been awarded a Silver Star and a Purple Heart and they were pinned on him by the Vice President himself at a reception at the V.A. hospital. The article stated he was discharged and had plans for a second career in the public sector. Raine knew a Purple Heart meant he'd been injured. She figured he must have post-traumatic stress disorder or something you couldn't see, because with the way that suit and wool coat hung on him, no one could tell her there was something wrong with his body.

She sighed and pulled her own coat tighter. The last person on earth Raine needed to be thinking about was Gage Jordan, but she couldn't help it. He was the jock she'd had a crush on in high school, the soldier she'd shared her first dance with and the only man she'd ever had a date with.

She smiled at the memory of that dance. His mother, whom she'd been talking to when he made his approach from across the room, had thrown them together. Raine remembered he'd had a determined look on his face, no doubt on a mission to convey some message. He whispered in is mother's ear and then before Evelyn Jordan left she handed her off to him and said firmly, "This pretty young woman has been holding up the wall for too long. Dance with her, son." Gage didn't hesitate to invite her to the floor. After all, the disc jockey was playing Brown Sugar. Even a confirmed gospel music only addict like Raine knew that song. Less than sixty seconds after they moved onto the dance floor, the tempo of the music slowed down and *If Only*

For One Night by Luther Vandross reverberated through the D.J.'s speakers.

"You don't mind this song, do you?" he asked. She surmised the question was a mere courtesy, because Gage took liberties before she could respond. He placed his hand on the small of her back and pulled her closer to him. Raine saw her life flash before her, but not in a way that scared one to death. Her own wedding, marriage, and children came to her in flashes of light. In those five minutes, she lived every dream she had ever had. And then Gage disappeared into the cabin of a military flight to a war thousands of miles away. She thought she'd never see him again.

A biting slice of the night air snatched her from her memory. She beat herself up for the long ago fantasy and continued the walk to her own car. She climbed in, turned the key and after a minute angrily banged on the steering wheel. It wouldn't start.

Chapter 4

Gage had been looking for her during the performance. He wished he'd had a set of those vision goggles they used on night raids. The place was so dark. The only light came from the small spotlights over their heads and then of course the stage.

He couldn't stop thinking about her. He knew it was silly, but Raine Still's eyes had awakened something in him and set a plan in motion. He had to know if she was here with a man. He was determined to find out. He needed to know if she was involved with someone, because he had too many regrets about what could have been.

Gage excused himself, exited the theater, and counted himself a lucky man when he saw her moving through the parking lot. She was alone. He hurried across the street where he spotted her. She was sitting in a PT Cruiser, arms wrapped around the steering wheel. Her head rested against it as well. He wondered if she was sick, but before he could ponder it more, she raised her head, opened the car door, and stepped out. That's when their eyes connected. For the third time tonight, his heartbeat sped up and his stomach dropped.

"Are you okay?" he asked, stepping closer.

Raine seemed stunned that he was speaking to her. She was frozen, her body half in the car and half out, clutching the door with one hand and her purse with the other. She watched him suspiciously as he closed the distance between them. Gage wondered if the reason she hadn't moved was because she was scared. She appeared to be using the car door as a shield. For that reason, he stopped walking. "You had your head down. I was wondering if you were okay?"

She opened her mouth to speak and then closed it like she wasn't sure how to answer the question. He didn't think it was a hard one, so he repeated it.

"I'm fine. I'm on my way back in," she replied in a silky tone that instantly warmed the cold night air.

"On your way back in? You looked like you were leaving."

She didn't reply. She just stood there mute, again. He smiled a bit and thought maybe he should use sign language, but decided teasing wasn't in order. "Are you going back to meet your friend?"

She shook her head. "No, actually, I need to call the auto club. I was going to wait inside. My car won't start."

Relief washed over him. Then Gage felt ashamed, because that pleased him for three reasons. One, it meant she wasn't ill. Two, she wasn't with a man, and three it gave him something to do for her. "Let me have a look."

"No, I couldn't." She shook her head quickly and repeatedly. "I can call."

"It'll only take a minute. Besides it's cold out here and they'll take an hour. The show is almost over. This place will be deserted soon."

He guessed she realized he was right because she took her other leg out of the car, handed him the key, and stepped back. The night air carried her sweet perfume straight to his nostrils. The scent nearly knocked him to his knees. Gage pulled himself together, got in the car and turned the ignition. The engine was dead. It didn't turn over at all. He pulled the lever to release the hood, stepped back out of the car and around it to take a look. The engine was clean, so it was well cared for. He craned his neck to look at some areas that were more hidden, but didn't see anything out of place.

"It may be your battery," he offered.

Raine sighed. "The door was open a bit when I came to it. I might have run it down."

"Let me get my truck. I'll give it a jump."

She started shaking her head again. "No, I couldn't impose that way. You're with your family."

Gage dismissed her protest. "It's no problem. I'm not much of a theater man anyway."

She dropped her head like she was embarrassed and said, "I'll wait here."

Gage's heart smiled. He practically ran to his truck, jumped in and pulled it around to the front of her vehicle. Before he stepped out, he sent Cree a text message to explain his absence. He was the second to the oldest, with Chase being the firstborn, but his sisters worried over him like he was the baby of the family. He let her know he was outside helping Raine with her car. Then he got out, opened the lift gate for the trunk, and took out the jumper cables he stored.

"I'm glad you have those, because I don't," Raine confessed.

He hooked the cables to his vehicles and then caught her eye as he passed her to attach them to hers. "You should. Anybody will give you a jump, but everybody doesn't have cables."

She shivered a bit and nodded. "I know. I've been taught better."

Gage frowned. "You're cold. Let me help you into my truck. The heat comes up pretty quick, so after I start it, it should be warm."

Raine smiled. Her teeth chattered through the lie on her

lips. "I'm not that cold. I can wait."

Gage connected the cables to his charging poles and then to hers. He started his car and then he tried to start hers. It was still dead.

"We'll let it run for a few minutes," he said.

Raine nodded, but after a few minutes, her car still would not start. He got out, disappointed that he couldn't rescue her.

"I don't know. How old is the battery? It may actually need to be replaced or it might be your starter."

Her shoulders slumped. "I can't believe this. I think I purchased that battery last year," she paused. "Well, maybe it was the year before that."

"No matter. We'll see about getting it towed. You call your auto club and I'll call my family to let them know what's going on."

Raine extended her swan like neck, a question in her eyes. "What is going on?"

Gage squinted through his amusement. "I'm waiting with you. I can't leave you alone out here."

"But, your family," she persisted.

"Arc all adults." He found himself amused again by her persistence. "Really, it's fine."

She rewarded him with a small smile that wordlessly thanked him.

"Now, let me help you into my truck. It's probably nice and toasty."

Raine pushed the key fob to lock her vehicle and walked around to the passenger side of the Hummer. Gage opened the door. They both paused for a moment before she slipped her hand in his. He noted how cold they were.

"Your hands are freezing. You were cold."

"My hands are always cold," she replied, dismissively.

He didn't remember them being cold when he'd touched them years ago, but it was spring then. He smiled. "Cold hands are good."

"Good." She cocked an eyebrow. "Why would you say that?"

"Cold hands, warm heart." Gage looked down into her eyes. He noticed her lashes fluttering nervously. *More blushing,* he thought and again he was moved by the appeal of it. He helped her into the vehicle. Raine slid into the seat and swept her coat tail in behind her. Once again their eyes met and Gage knew if she had a man, he didn't mean anything to her. Her eyes told the story. Satisfied, he closed the door and sent a text to Cree to let her know she, Brooke, and Arielle would be riding home in the limo with their parents.

Chapter 5

Gage Jordan was a gentleman in every sense of the word. Raine had never in her life felt so taken care of by a man that wasn't her father. She was thirty-four and ridiculously inexperienced. The only thing she knew about men and dating was what she'd learned on television and in novels and that scared her, because she was dangerously impressed with him; again already.

She turned her head away from him and stared out the window as he maneuvered the large vehicle and pulled it out of the parking lot. The theater was emptying. She caught sight of his brother, Cade, and his television star wife, or ex-television star. Raine couldn't remember the last show she'd seen her in or even heard she'd done. Cade had been a wide receiver for the *Atlanta Falcons* for two seasons before he was injured, so they were both exes.

She remembered the golden couple that they were at their wedding. It was one of many her mother had performed at over the years. The woman had a voice that brought heaven to earth until the day she closed her eyes. Now she was singing in heaven. Raine wanted to celebrate that, but she couldn't. Her own pain was too great.

Gage's melodic voice broke through her thoughts. "How long did the auto club tell you it would be?"

She let her eyes peruse his person. Strong hands gripped the steering wheel; large biceps filled his coat and that face...no woman could resist how blessed in the face he was. "An hour. Like you said."

Raine returned her gaze to the passing homes and cars outside her window. She couldn't believe that she was in the car with him. Four hours ago when she was getting dressed, she had resigned herself to spending the evening the way she always did. Alone. But here she was sitting in a Hummer, of all vehicles, with the most attractive man she had ever known.

Raine heard him playing with the buttons on the dash before she turned to see what he was doing. Through expertly tuned speakers, the sweet sound of Anita Baker's voice filled the vehicle.

After a minute of staring out the window while listening to *Been So Long* she said, "It's a little warm. Could you turn down the heat a bit?"

He chuckled like she'd said something funny. She wondered if he thought she was implying some kind of sexual innuendo by that statement since they were listening to a slow jam. She cringed inwardly and added. "This coat is cashmere." She glanced at him. Gage pulled his eyes away from the road and looked into hers. Then he pushed the button to reduce the heat.

"I'm sorry about that. My sisters like it a little warm. I think they all have low iron or something." He chuckled again. "I wanted you to be comfortable, but I was about to crack my window. I prefer cooler weather."

He continued to move through the streets and had begun to move out of the urban area where the theater was located into the downtown area. They had traveled a good distance from the theater. "Where are we going?"

"I've got a sweet tooth. I went to a dessert bar after dinner and didn't order anything, now I'm dying for some ice cream. I was thinking we had time to go to Queen's." His eyes and teeth gleamed in the darkness. "Do you like ice cream?"

A low chuckle escaped her lips. "Is that a trick question?"

"You know you have to be careful with Black folks. Most of us are lactose intolerant."

She laughed again. "I can still drink milk."

She wasn't looking at him, but she could feel his eyes on her.

"So, is it okay with you?"

Raine thought his warm, velvety voice would melt anything they served him at Queen's, but who was she to stand in the way of the man's sweet-tooth. "I like Queen's."

"Good, I'm jonesing for one of their banana splits."

"One of their splits? That's a lot of ice cream on a cold night like this."

"It'll be alright. I can remember sitting out in the cold desert at night wishing I could have some of Queen's ice cream. Now that I can, I'm not denying myself anything. Life is too short for that."

Raine let her eyes sweep his profile. "I guess it depends on the life you're living. Sometimes life seems unbearably long to me."

"Perspective plays a part in everything." He hesitated a moment and then said, "I heard my mother mention a funeral. I hope I don't upset you by asking, but who passed away?"

Raine took in a deep breath and let it out slowly. "Both my parents died last year."

She could see a frown cloud his face and then again his eyes were on her briefly. He pulled into the parking lot of Queen's and turned off the engine. "I'm sorry," he said. "I mean, how…"

She swallowed. She could feel her eyes getting wet. "My dad of natural causes in December. Not last month December, the previous year and then my mom passed in June. She'd been sick." Her voice sounded sad even to her.

The earnestness of his sympathy instantly filled the space in the car. "I'm really sorry to hear that, Raine. It must have been very hard for you to lose them both like that. I wish I had known."

She had been trying hard not to look at him, but now she did. His eyes were on her and the intensity of his gaze was unnerving. "It was a horrible year," she muttered darkly.

"What have you been doing to help yourself work through it?"

She was silenced by the question. No one had asked her that – not straight out like that. She shrugged. "I don't know. I guess taking things day by day. Trying not to spend too much of the day grieving."

He nodded like that was sufficient and then cut the engine. "That sounds like the right thing to do."

They sat there in the quiet for a moment. She dared not look back at him, but she could feel his eyes on her. After a minute, his car door opened and then he was opening hers. He took her hand again and this time she was less embarrassed because they weren't near as cold as they had been the first time. The warmth of their hands connecting jarred her. Raine almost lost her balance. Gage sensed it and wrapped an arm around her.

"Are you okay?" he asked. His breath was a whisper on her face.

She shook her head and raised her eyes to meet his. The last time she was this close to him they were in much the same position. His hand was on the small of her back. His eyes were so close to hers that the hypnotic pull was intensely disarming.

"You know if you ever need someone to talk to about your parents..."

Raine stepped out of his grasp and cleared her throat again. "That's generous of you." She knew her tone didn't match her words. She wasn't looking for amateur grief counseling. She certainly didn't want it from someone who didn't understand.

His forehead crinkled in confusion. "I'm not being generous. I'm a good listener is all."

"Is that something they taught you in the Army?"

Gage chuckled. "You learn patience in the Army. I'm not sure that helps in the area of attending skills, but I've had some training. I have my masters in counseling. I managed to finish it a few years ago." He paused for a moment and then added. "Not that I'm trying to play shrink or anything. I've experienced some loss, so I know that talking about it can help."

"And did you?" Even though she felt a little guilty about her tart tone, Raine continued to challenge him.

His eyebrows knit together. "Did I what?"

"Talk to someone?"

He smiled like he'd been caught not practicing what he preached. "A few times."

"Did it help?" she pressed, thinking about her best friend's insistence that she see someone herself.

"Not really, but I may have been talking to the wrong person." He swallowed hard because she noted how exaggerated his Adam's apple had grown. A knot of pain, she surmised. Raine knew that swallow well.

Gage closed the open vehicle door with a push, signaling the end of their tense conversation and said, "They're closing in like twenty minutes, so let's get in there and place an order."

They were in and out of Queen's quickly as the wiping of tables and mopping of the floor had begun. Gage ordered a caramel and brownie banana split and Raine a cup of espresso and a chocolate donut. He was just about to help her into his truck when she heard her name.

"Raine Still."

That was the second time tonight. She supposed this is what happened when a person got out of the house. Clara Mayer, one of her coworkers and another woman stepped up to them.

Clara looked her up and down like she couldn't believe she was dressed up. She frowned and in a sickly, pitchy tone said, "I hardly recognized you."

Raine didn't know how she recognized her either since her eyes were now locked on Gage.

He smiled, revealing two impossibly handsome dimples and introduced himself. "Gage Jordan." He looked from Clara to Raine and added, "I'm guessing you don't wear formal attire to work, so the dress is a different look."

The comment was spoken to her but directed at the mean girl. Raine smiled. She wasn't sure if Clara even got what he was saying. She was so busy checking him and his car out.

"Where are you coming from," Clara asked, unbuttoning her coat to reveal her large, barely covered breast in the skimpy top she wore. If Gage noticed her chest, he was a pro at ignoring it.

"The Show," Raine replied. "Have you heard of it?"

Clara grimaced. "Of course, but who can get tickets?"

Gage smiled. "We did." He pointed toward Queen's.

"You might want to get in there. They'll probably lock the door behind you."

Clara nodded and said, "See you at the staff meeting next week, Raine. Nice to meet you, Gage."

Then they were gone, chattering as they entered the restaurant.

Raine realized she would be the talk of the office on Monday. *Plain Raine was out with the hottest hunk in Charlotte on Saturday night.* She smiled inwardly. That kind of talk might not be a bad thing.

"Let's go." He opened the back door and sat the bag on the backseat.

Raine smiled at him. For a moment, Gage looked confused.

"What did I do to deserve that smile?"

She shrugged. "You stood up for me. I'm not used to anyone doing that."

"Women can be mean to each other. I've seen it a lot. I've heard my sisters talk about it," he said. "And I'm quick on my feet."

"Sarcasm can be a gift I suppose."

He frowned. "Not really. I'm not sure God intended for us to talk to each other sarcastically."

"I think Jesus was a little sarcastic in the parables. At least He was in my Bible."

Gage laughed heartily. "So are you thinking what would Jesus do? Say something snarky."

"I bet he would," she replied.

"I'm not sure about that either." He took her hand. Again she felt electricity pass between them. Raine thought Gage must have as well, because he looked affected too.

Raine thought she could get in and out of this car all night if it meant she got to touch him.

He cleared his throat. "We'd better hurry. We have less than twenty minutes until the auto club will be there."

They were parked next to her car before the twenty minutes was up. While she finished her coffee, she watched Gage eat his ice cream. He was as excited as a five year-old. Raine would have found it amusing if her mind didn't drift to the reason it was probably such a big deal to him; the sacrifice of deployment.

She drilled him as he ate. She was shocked to find out he had been deployed three more times since the last time she'd seen him, twice to Iraq and to Afghanistan on his last tour . She asked him about the weather, the food, his daily routine and what he liked most and hated most about deployment. Before she knew it they had been talking for an hour. Raine yawned and Gage said, "I better get you home."

Heaviness caused her shoulders to fall. "I can't believe they didn't come."

"They may have lost the call or they could still be on the way. You should cancel. I'll bring you back in the morning. I have a battery charger. We can try that. If it that doesn't work, you can get the tow then."

She supposed that made sense, but said instead, "I don't want to inconvenience you by having you pick me up and come back. I live in the Southpark area."

Gage turned to put his trash on the seat behind him. "I don't mind. I don't have anything to do. I go to church, but I'd already planned to attend the late service."

His offer was so generous Raine hardly knew what to say, so she just said, "Thank you."

Dimples shown in the dark. He whispered, "My pleasure."

She gave him her address. Gage put it in his navigation system and they pulled out of the parking lot for the second time that evening.

"I hope I'm not taking you too far out of your way," she said.

"You're not. I'm in Myers Park. On the south end."

She raised an eyebrow. "Myers Park is nice."

He chuckled. "I'm staying with Brooke. I'll be renting from her soon. She'll be moving to New Jersey in two weeks. She's engaged to a man that lives there and her job transfer came through."

Raine clasped her hands together and looked down at them. It must be nice to have a future, she thought, but said, "That's great for her. Please tell her I said congratulations."

She could see him nod in her peripheral vision.

They rode in silence to her house. The sugar Gage ingested seemed to have dulled his chattiness. The trip wasn't long and traffic was nonexistent. His navigation brought them right to her door. He cut the engine.

Gage looked through the window past Raine. "This is a nice house. Nice neighborhood. You were looking the last time we talked."

She had been house-hunting that spring. She'd found this one the very week he'd left. She inspected the shrubs that needed pruning and the trim that needed a fresh coat of paint. She'd neglected her house during her mother's illness. "Thank you."

"How long have you been here?"

"Six years. It was a foreclosure during the early run of foreclosures. I'd finished my master's degree and gotten a promotion at work, so I thought, it was time."

"I remember you'd just finished your masters. You

mentioned it that day."

His memory was impeccable. Raine's stomach flipped. That day. That day she'd shared a table with him in the mall food court because all the others were full. That day lunch turned into a trip to the movie theatre, dinner and a stroll through a bookstore.

"No waiting for a husband to buy a house with, huh?" he asked, but then he didn't wait for an answer. "I like that. The women in my family are very independent too."

Gage smiled. It sucked the wind out of her. Not because he was so good looking, or even because he had flashed his movie star, picture ready white teeth, it was the disposition behind the smile. Lazy, relaxed…Raine didn't exactly know the word she was looking for. He seemed interested in her, again. He wasn't making small talk to fill up the time, because they were here at her house. All he had to do was open the door and then open hers and walk her to the door of her house, if he was so inclined to do that. In seconds, he could be done with Raine Still for tonight and forever. But Gage wasn't moving. He wasn't trying to leave.

The only man that had ever been interested in her was her father. He'd hung on to every word she'd said from the time she could talk until he took his last breath. But this attention from Gage was different. She didn't know how to take it. She'd been here with him before and then he disappeared without a trace.

"Can I ask you a question?" His tone was tentative. "What happened to your date tonight?"

Raine had no idea what he would ask, but this question surprised her. "I didn't have a date."

Gage's expression posed the follow-up question before he did. "You said you were waiting for someone."

She shrugged. "I lied. I wanted to be alone and I thought

it was easier to say I was waiting on someone than be rude to all of you."

He cocked an eyebrow. "That's honest."

"I don't like to lie and I don't have any reason to lie to you now."

"Why did you have so many tickets if you weren't expecting anyone?"

Raine couldn't keep the amusement out of her voice. "Are you questioning if I'm lying about lying?"

A beautiful crooked smile filled half his face, revealing one of his dimples. "I'm not questioning if you're lying. I guess I'm just curious, nosy."

Raine explained how she came to have the extra tickets. Gage nodded. "That was God. You were supposed to help us out."

Raine didn't think that made any sense. "Why wouldn't God just make it so I had one ticket and your mother had the ones she needed?"

Silence again and then, "Because if God made it happen that way then I wouldn't have run into you."

She swallowed now. Hard. He was staring at her. Looking from her face to her lips. He leaned closer and put a hand behind her neck. Then he brought his face closer so that it hovered just inches from hers. Raine could smell his breathe, the mint he'd popped into his mouth after eating the ice cream. She could also smell his cologne, a strong, sexy masculine scent that rose from his pores to torment her.

But then just as quickly as he'd pulled her close, Gage let her go and reached for his ignition key. "It's late. I need to get you inside."

Get her inside. She didn't have a curfew. Raine was disappointed. But more than disappointed, she was embarrassed. She wanted that kiss. "I can see myself to my door," she replied, icily. She released her seat belt and grabbed the door handle.

His hand was on hers. "Raine, let me explain."

She turned toward him and frowned. "Explain what?"

"Why I stopped."

Raine thought she would die. No he was not going to explain why he was rejecting her. She sighed heavily.

"I don't want to be disrespectful."

The conversation was awkward, but he'd started it, so she questioned, "A kiss is disrespectful?"

He didn't remove his hand from hers, but he didn't respond either.

Oh my God, she thought. *He has a girlfriend or maybe even a wife.* Of course he did. How could she be so naïve? He didn't want to disrespect his marriage. She dropped her eyes to their intertwined fingers. So why was he still holding her hand?

He finally spoke. "I'm careful about what I start."

That only confused her more. "What does that mean?" she whispered. And then she thought, I don't want to know. "Never mind. You don't have to explain." She grabbed the door handle again, but Gage squeezed the hand he held. She froze.

"I do, because I don't want you to think I didn't want to kiss you. My stopping has nothing to do with you."

Raine didn't look at him. If she could have jumped out of the car and run in the house without seeming rude she would have. She wanted to escape the pounding rush in her veins. The agony over the fact that the only man she'd ever wanted was taken. "Of course, I understand. You have to respect your wife or your girlfriend."

"Wife or girlfriend?" She could hear a frown in his voice.

"You've been a real gentleman, Gage. I appreciate the ride."

"Wait," he insisted. "I don't have a wife or a girlfriend."

Raine knew she should not let the next question come out of her mouth because it was embarrassing and it would sound like begging, but she would drive herself crazy if she didn't know. Since she knew she'd never see him again, she went ahead asked, "Then why did you stop?"

The expression on his face was so serious it nearly looked pained. "It's late." He released her hand. "I'll be back in the morning."

"In the morning?"

"I told you I was picking you up so we could see about getting your car started or towed."

She shook her head. "It is really kind of you to offer, but you don't have to do that."

His words came swift and impulsively. "What if I want to do it?"

Her stomach flipped again. "Why would you want to do it? We're not neighbors."

"For the same reason I didn't kiss you. I finish what I start. Once I commit to a thing, I have to see it all the way through."

He smiled and opened his door. Once she got out they fell into step up her long walkway. She said good night to her prince, pushed the door closed and peeked out to watch him disappear. Raine kicked off her shoes and realized the irony of having both shoes. She hadn't left one behind, so the prince didn't have one. Gage didn't have a reason to come looking for her. He didn't even have anything to look with, because he hadn't even asked for her phone number to call to make arrangements for tomorrow. Her Cinderella story was a bust.

Chapter 6

It was seven a.m. on a Sunday morning. Clearly a rude time to knock on anyone's door, but he was here and there was no going back, so Gage rang the doorbell.

He waited three minutes and rang it again. Raine was probably asleep and who knew how hard she did that. Gage couldn't believe he hadn't gotten her telephone number last night. He hadn't been thinking about anything but getting away from her before he went too far. Now he regretted his hasty exit, because he'd have to wait in the car or go home and come back. He had turned to go back to his car to contemplate what he would do next when he heard the door open.

Raine stuck her head out. Bed hair framed her face. "Gage," she said his name like she couldn't believe it was him.

"Sorry I didn't call first. I didn't get your number last night. You're not listed."

Raine pulled the door open a little more. She was wearing a robe that she pulled tight around her. But Gage had already stolen a glance at her pajama shorts. They hit her mid-thigh on her long legs. Lingerie was nice, but short pjs like that were just as sexy. He was a leg man and at 5'8 or better, Raine had them for days. He cleared his throat. "I'm military so I get up early. Seven is nearly lunchtime."

Raine raised her hand to her hair and smoothed it. He could tell she was feeling self-conscious.

"Look, why don't I go get a cup of coffee while you get

dressed. What do you need?" A vision of his laboriously slow sisters flittered through his mind, so Gage decided to put a time limit on the getting ready. "Will thirty minutes be enough?"

She shook her head. "You came all this way. It's generous of you to even do this. I can be ready in fifteen minutes." She pulled the door open all the way. "Come in. You can have a seat while I get dressed."

Gage stepped in. He did a quick sweep of her living room. He suddenly felt like he was back in college, in European history. The room had a Bohemian flair to it. The colors were a mix of blood red and forest greens, nicely contrasted with yellows and gold. She had a brick wall treatment. Her artwork depicted the Bohemian era of the nineteenth century. There was even a stained glass lantern hanging over the coffee table. It was different, but nice and not surprising considering her parents had been known to be hippies of a sort.

"I apologize again for being so early. I was hoping to catch the noon service at church and then there's football, so I figured…"

She pulled the knot on her robe tighter. "It's no problem. I mean, it's not like its five a.m."

He chuckled. "I get up at five, so I really waited it out."

Silence hung between them. A beeping sound interrupted the awkward pause. Gage remembered hearing the sound when he first walked in, but thought it might be some kind of motion detector chime. He looked around and noticed the light on the smoke detector was red. "Do you have a battery? I could change that while you get dressed."

She picked a remote up off the table. "I'll take care of it when I get back. You can make yourself comfortable."

"Are you sure?" he pressed. "I don't watch much T.V.

so, if you have a battery and a screw driver I can make myself useful."

Raine hesitated for a moment and then disappeared into the kitchen. She returned with a screwdriver and a double pack of 9-volt batteries and handed them to him. "That's sweet of you," she said. Their eyes locked for a moment, the same way they'd connected last night. Raine turned her head. The blush in her cheeks deepened and she headed up the stairs. "I'll be back in a few minutes." She called down when she reached the top.

Gage turned his attention to the smoke detector. He recognized the type. They were the same brand Jordan Homes used in all their new construction. That's why he knew he needed a screwdriver. He switched out the battery and pushed the button to reset it. The alarm sounded. Raine yelled down the stairs, "Is everything okay?"

"Just testing it!"

Gage laid the screwdriver down on the sofa table. Just as he was about to sit, he heard the same beep come from another room. He'd seen that before with this system. They were wired so that all the batteries would have to be changed at the same time. He picked up the screwdriver and the leftover battery and walked in the direction he'd heard the beep. As he was moving it beeped again. Now he was positive it was coming from a room ahead. It was a small sitting room. He fancied it a woman cave, the opposite of a man cave because it was full of books and candles. A collection of Barbie dolls and Raine's old school, vinyl albums and compact disc music collection were stored here. The other end of the room, however, was configured like a home office with a two monitor set up, printers, scanners and short file cabinets. He noted the offending smoke detector over a small writing desk.

Gage frowned as he approached the table. There was an open bottle of prescription pills and a glass of water on the table. All the pills were lined up on the desk like someone had been playing with them or counting them. And then there was a note.

Dear Kiara,

I'm so sorry you're reading this letter. I want you to know you've been the best friend I could ever hope for, so please don't blame yourself because I decided doing this was best for me. I…

And then it ended. Ended like she'd been interrupted. There was a stamped envelope next to it addressed to Kiara Snow with a Phoenix address.

Gage's stomach twisted from the bile that rose. Raine was suicidal. How was that possible?

He picked up the battery and backed out of the room. He couldn't change the detector in there. She'd know he'd seen the letter and the pills and that would… What? He asked himself. Embarrass her? Wasn't it better to embarrass her than not talk about what she was planning? He felt sick at the thought. He hurried back into the great room area and put the screwdriver and battery on the table like he'd been a good houseguest and not discovered her secret.

A minute later, Raine came down the stairs. She was dressed in jeans and a sweater. Her long silky hair hung around her shoulders like black strands of glass. There had been no time for makeup and she certainly didn't need it. She was beautiful and vibrant and radiant. It made him sad to think underneath it all she was dying inside, but Gage was glad he knew her secret. He could help her.

"You look great," he said.

She pulled her head back like she didn't believe him, but thanked him for the compliment.

"Another one of your detectors is beeping. It sounds

like it's coming from back there. Did you want me to get it?"

She looked toward the opening to the room he'd just exited. Sadness filled her eyes for a moment and she shook her head. "I'll take care of it when I get back."

Although he thought he should, he didn't push this time. He would wait for another opportunity.

They exited the house. Raine turned the key in the deadbolt and asked, "Do you know of an auto shop that will be open this early?"

Her car wasn't that old, but he reasoned it had to be at least five years old. "You don't have a mechanic?" he asked, thinking she should with an older vehicle.

"Not really. The men at Hope House were handy with cars and so was my dad. I let them fix it. This is my first time having car trouble since..."

"Hope House?" His tone asked the question.

"It's a transitional housing place that," she paused and stopped herself.

"Raine," he said pulling her back from the place she seemingly had disappeared to.

"I'm sorry. My father and some friends of his did the work on my car."

Satisfied with her answer, Gage dropped the subject and didn't push about Hope House. He helped her into the truck. "I have my battery charger. If it's the battery, a charge might bring it back." He started the engine and drove in the direction of the Plaza-Midwood area where the theater was.

He pushed the button for the radio. Praise music filtered in on low through the speakers. They drove in silence for most of the way. Gage had to fight hard to keep from asking Raine about the pills and the note. He cast a glance at her and again was struck by how beautiful she was and not just

59

physically. It wasn't like people who were mediocre could go kill themselves. No, it was her inner beauty. Her soul was beautiful. He couldn't imagine someone that cast so much light being filled with enough darkness to take their own life.

"So, Raine, do you go to worship on Sunday?"

She hesitated before answering, "I used to. I have to admit it's been a few months. I always attended the church my parents went to. Now going there reminds me of their funerals. I don't know. It makes me sad."

He nodded. "You probably need a new beginning. You're welcome to join me. I attend Greater Christian Faith. It's a little out of your way, up near Freedom Drive, but worth the travel."

"Thank you for the invitation. I'll keep it in mind."

Silence filled the vehicle. Gage wondered what Raine was thinking about. Where did her mind stray when living had become so unimportant?

"So, do you have any other relatives in Charlotte?" he asked.

"I don't have any relatives period. Not that I know of."

Gage couldn't imagine that. His heart ached for her. His family was such an integral part of his life.

"I'm adopted as you may have guessed." She smiled.

He half-smiled and glanced at her. "I was thinking those two elderly White folks hadn't had you naturally, but then there was a couple named Abraham and Sarah."

Raine smiled at Gage's joke. "They started off as my foster parents. I was in state custody from the time I was two months old. My natural mother or parents or whomever, left me in a hospital waiting room. Anyway, my mom volunteered at the hospital. She was there when they found me and because she had a licensed foster home, she got to take me home. Once I was available for adoption they made it permanent."

He couldn't help but appraise her with his gaze. Such a sad story, but she told it with joy and admiration for the people who has raised her. "Bouncing around in the foster care system wouldn't have been good. I know you're glad you dodged that bullet."

"I was blessed. They were good to me. I wouldn't have wanted anyone else to raise me."

"What about their family?"

"They were both only children. My dad has a couple of cousins, but I never met them. They are all dead now. My parents outlived everyone."

Interesting, he thought. He'd never even considered not having family. He'd met a few men over the years who had little family, but there was usually someone even if it was someone they didn't like. She was lonely and grieving. He understood that. But lonely enough to take her life?

You're judging her. A voice in his heart said. He shrank back a bit from shame.

They pulled off Hwy 16, made a few turns and headed towards Central Avenue where the theatre was located. They stopped along the way and grabbed some coffee and bagels. Raine's car was one of two in the lot. Gage parked and got out of his truck. Raine followed. She attempted to start her vehicle again as he instructed her, but it was still dead. Gage hooked the portable battery charger up to it and they got back in his truck.

They ate breakfast. Raine asked questions about his transition out of the military and what his future plans were. That was a difficult conversation for him to have, but it wasn't a difficult one to have with her.

"I loved being in the Army. Being out now is hard. It's

hard for me to think about doing anything else."

Concern etched her face. "You can't go back, I guess."

"My knee is shot. I can't run. A soldier has to be able to do that."

"You don't walk with a limp."

"I do a little when I'm exhausted," he replied.

Raine looked at him like that grieved her. It touched him deep in the pit of his stomach. She seemed to have a straight shot to that spot.

"How did you get hurt," she asked.

He wasn't ready to answer that question, so he was glad to be able to say the full light was lit on the charger. Gage hopped out of the truck, disconnected the charger and had Raine turn over the engine. It started.

Raine popped out of the Hummer and clapped her hands. "Thank you so much," she said, as she threw her arms around him.

The sweet smell of her freshly showered body fired his nerves like the spark plugs that charged her car. Her sudden closeness sent his heart into frenzied palpitations. Gage swallowed hard. Raine stepped back, her expression filled with joy over the car. *She is so easy to please.* He thought to himself.

"You saved me," she said.

"Saved you from what," Gage asked, thinking he'd like to save her from death, but saying. "All I saved you from was a rental car." He was still trying to recover from the hug that had jolted him. He picked up the charger and put it in the back of his truck.

"I appreciate not having to get a rental," she said, pulling her jacket closer around her neck and then rubbing her ungloved hands together.

"I'll give you my number. Just in case you have any more trouble out of it. You can call me. I know a great mechanic and he's about halfway between your house and mine."

They both got their cell phones from the Hummer and exchanged telephone numbers. She thanked him again. Raine slammed her car door. His heart slammed in his chest. His time with her had been the sweet reward of being a Good Samaritan, but it had been too short.

Gage watched the little PT Cruiser pull out of the parking lot. He couldn't help but think he missed her already. He didn't want to let her go and would she be alright.

Chapter 7

Raine knew it was silly, but she almost wished her car hadn't started. If it hadn't, she'd still be with Gage. She would be enjoying his conversation, listening to his voice, soaking in his masculinity, and admiring his...well, admiring him she thought and giggled out loud to herself like a silly schoolgirl. Her cell phone alarmed. She noted it was the tone for a reminder app. The one she used to make sure she didn't miss important dates. She reached for it and swiped the screen. "Hope" was all that was displayed. Raine sighed. She had to make a decision. The clock was running out on Hope House and she honestly didn't know what to do.

Her phone rang, startling her. She recognized the image of her friend, Kiara, on the screen and answered.

"This was going to be my last call before I got on a plane," Kiara yelled. Thanks to Bluetooth technology, her voice filled the cabin of the small SUV. "Why are you not answering my calls?"

Raine chuckled. "You were not going to get on a plane. You don't fly."

"I was going to make myself," Kiara replied. "What is going on? I've been calling you for weeks."

"I'm sorry. I've been...busy."

"Too busy to send a text."

"I'm sorry. I'm just..."

Kiara sighed on the other end. "Honey, you can't do this."

Moisture clouded her vision. "I'm not doing anything."

"Did you call like you promised you would?"

Raine shook her head. She had not called the therapist and she had no reason why she hadn't. Just that she had given up. She hated hearing the pain in Kiara's voice, probably as much as Kiara hated hearing it in hers.

"It was better when you were here."

"But I can't come back, honey and you won't consider moving, so…"

Raine sniffed. She felt like a fool. Kiara was a newlywed. She wasn't responsible for her happiness. She had no right to even make her feel this way. "Kiara, I'm better."

Silence.

"You're not," Kiara said, "and I'm so worried about you."

"Don't worry."

"I am. I just wish you'd help yourself. Counseling doesn't mean crazy."

"I know that. My father was a counselor, remember."

"So, why can't you just call her and go?" Kiara pressed.

Because she didn't want help, Raine thought. She wanted to be with her parents. There was nothing here for her. A therapist couldn't change that.

"It doesn't have to stay the way it is," Kiara stole her thoughts from her head. "Counselors give coping strategies. You need to learn how to cope. Once you do that, then you can begin to do some things. A hobby or a book club or something. You've been taking care of people your entire life."

Tears flowed freely now. Her nose began to run. A car horn blared behind her and she realized she'd been sitting at a green light.

"What's that noise?" Kiara asked.

Raine got her bearings and moved through the light and turned onto Tryon Street.

"You're out. Are you going to church?" The excitement in her friend's voice was palpable. Church could fix it. That's what Kiara believed. That's what her mother taught her. *Jesus Will Fix It*, had been her mother's favorite hymn. Raine heard it playing in her mind.

"Are you going to Oak Hill?" Kiara asked, mentioning her former church. "Or trying someplace new?"

It would be so easy to lie. Kiara would be thrilled. She wouldn't be worried about her. But she didn't lie to Kiara. Not ever. And Raine didn't want to lie about going to church. "I'm going to Hope. I have to decide what I'm going to do."

"And have you?" Kiara's voice held hope of it's own.

"No."

"I don't know how you can even think about letting it go. Even if you don't reopen the place right now, you can pay the taxes and hold on to it."

"I've paid to board it up five times. It's costing me too much to keep it empty and it'll cost me too much to open it."

"Raine, is this really about money? There are grants and donations for places like Hope."

Frustration filled her tone. "You talk about me having a new beginning, but then you want me to keep Hope. How is that a new beginning?"

"I don't know," Kiara said. "I don't have all the answers, but I do know God can show you how to make it brand new."

Kiara's words did nothing to ease Raine's guilt.

"I don't want you to have regrets. I don't want you to look up a year from now and hate yourself for not choosing to keep the place. I don't think you'll be able to live with yourself if you let it go."

I wasn't planning on living with myself, she thought. I wasn't going to live at all. Raine signaled and glanced in her rearview mirror to make sure she could move into the right lane. That's when she saw the black Hummer in the distance.

"What's he doing?" she asked, audibly.

"He who?" Kiara was quick to respond to the word "he". She always had been.

"Gage Jordan."

"Gage." Kiara was silent for a few seconds. "I remember that name. Is that the guy from your high school? The one you went on that date with?"

"Yes," Raine replied, knowing Kiara had a memory like an entire safari of elephants. She never forgot a name.

"Okay." Kiara sang the word. "What are you doing with him?"

"He's following me."

"Following you?"

"It's a long story," Raine said, pulling into a parking spot in front of Hope House. She looked out at the two building structure, taking in the litter in the yard, peeling trim, and the biggest black eye of all, the burned out window on the upper-level.

"I have time for a story. Sounds like some stuff has been going on back there. No wonder you're not calling."

Raine pursed her lips. "Nothing is going on."

"You said he's following you. That's something. He's

not crazy is he?"

Raine shook her head, like Kiara could see her. "No. He just helped me with my car. It wouldn't start and now, he's behind me. Look. I have to go. I'll explain later."

"Hmmm…" Kiara purred. "So much more energy in your voice. Is he still single?"

"Kiara, I'll call you." This time Raine was firmer.

"Do not make me fly to Charlotte. I want to hear from you tonight."

"I will call." Raine turned off the car and the phone switched to the handset.

She heard Kiara say bye, then the connection ended.

She looked back and watched Gage park his truck behind her.

"Well, you wanted to see him again," she whispered to herself. She pushed her small handbag under the seat, grabbed the keys and stepped out of the car.

Chapter 8

A Hummer was not the vehicle to drive when you wanted to be inconspicuous, so of course she knew he was behind her. Gage thought he should be embarrassed about following her, but he wasn't. At this point, however, he was feeling like a stalker. She'd thanked him for his help, they'd said their goodbyes, and gone their separate ways. He intended to let that be it, until he noticed Raine was heading north, not south toward her house. He was headed north also, toward I-85 to get to the other side of Charlotte where his parent's church was, so technically, he wasn't following her, they'd just been going in the same direction. Then he saw her turn on Tryon Street. Tryon led to one of the roughest neighborhoods in Charlotte. He couldn't help thinking that was a mistake. And he didn't want that mistake to happen when she was in a vehicle that had proved to be unreliable less than twenty-four hours ago.

He met her on the sidewalk, quickly observing the sign that hung sideways on a post at the end of the walkway. Hope House. Now Gage was glad he had followed her. It was possible she was going to need him and God help him, he wanted to feel needed.

"I promise I'm not stalking you."

Raine smiled. He thought he'd never seen her eyes look sadder. They were filled with tears. "I don't feel like I'm being stalked at all," she said. "You keep showing up when I need someone."

Gage thought his heart would burst in his chest. Whatever this place was, it was intensely personal and he was glad she wasn't going through it alone when she was so fragile. Raine seemed frozen and confused, like she hadn't considered the next step once she arrived. "You want to go inside?" he asked.

She shrugged like she wasn't sure.

"I'll tell you what. Let's put one foot in front of the other until we reach the door and then you can decide what you want to do from there."

Raine dropped her head again. Gage took a hand, placed it under her chin, and tipped it up. "I'm here."

"I don't understand why?"

"Because I'm supposed to be." He rubbed a finger along her jawline. She raised her hand to cover his for a moment and then shifted from under his touch.

She reached into her pocket, removed a set of keys and placed them in his hand. With her other hand she saluted him and whispered, "At your command, Captain."

He laughed at her teasing and said, "I'll play. Forward march."

She fell into step with him.

Gage couldn't reconcile how good she felt next to him with how long he'd actually known her. This was the second time he'd had this feeling around Raine Still. Even in the cold he could feel the heat radiating off her body. It felt good to have a woman next to him that wasn't his mother or sister or a physical therapist or nurse or even under his command. He put the key in the main lock, turned it and pushed the door open. Then with a hand on her lower back, he physically guided Raine inside.

The inside was much like the outside. It needed a paint job, windows repaired and some repairs to the holes in the wall. But it wasn't bad. There was still furniture and no one had removed the few inexpensive paintings from the walls.

Raine seemed transfixed at the entrance. Gage imagined all kinds of memories were coming back to her.

"This is the housing for the women," she said. "This is where I spent most of my time. I went to the house for the men when I wanted to visit my father. It's the house next door."

Gage hadn't realized the two houses were connected, but he guessed he should have since the sign was in the middle.

Raine stepped toward the fireplace and looked up at a painting of an eagle embossed with words from Isaiah Chapter 40, verse 31. *But those who hope in the Lord will renew their strength. They will soar on wings like eagles; they will run and not grow weary; they will walk and not be faint.*

She extended her hand and stopped just short of touching the frame. "This was my dad's favorite scripture. He posted it here to remind the residents that there was always hope if they put their faith in God."

Gage stepped closer to her. "I've relied on it to encourage me on many a night. It's a powerful word."

"They named the ministry Hope because of it."

Gage nodded. "How did your parents get this place started?"

Raine bit down on her lower lip for a moment, closed her eyes and moaned before opening them again. "On a dream and a prayer they said. Both of them had had periods of homelessness when they were teenagers. My father's father was a drinker. He put my dad out of his house the day after he graduated high school. My father said he slept in the park one night, a mission for a few weeks and then he finally decided to join the Army. He knew he'd have a bed there." Raine's chuckle was void of laughter. "My mother had a similar story. Her mother remarried when she was sixteen. Her stepfather tried to rape her one night and instead of calling the police her mother asked her to leave. Sent her out the door with her clothes and school books." Raine's eyes got misty. "Can you imagine that? Their parents turning their children out because they were an inconvenience."

Gage shook his head. "Not really, but I know we had a lot of young enlisted with us because they had no place to go."

She sighed. "Anyway, my dad served in the Korean War. He came back and started working at a textile plant near the airport. My mother worked there too. She was a dye girl. That's what they called the women who handled the color matching near the dye vats." Raine began to walk through the house. Gage followed, but kept his distance enough to allow her to explore on her own. She wasn't tearful anymore, just reminiscent.

"They got married and saved for their world travels. When they had enough money they started camping all over the country. They even went to Europe. They found homelessness to be a problem all over the U.S. and in Europe, so they decided they wanted to do something about it. When they came back to Charlotte they did." She paused near a rocking chair and sat down. Raine closed her eyes and rocked back and forth a few times like sitting in it transported her to a place far, far away, but close to her heart. She opened her eyes and said, "My father made this chair."

Gage was impressed. "He had a gift in woodwork."

Raine smiled and stood. "A self-taught carpenter," she said. "Anyway, they rented this house and found the homeless downtown and at the family and children services office. My dad picked up men at the V.A. hospital. Finding tenants was never a problem. When the second house became available they rented that one too and then the owner died and his son sold both houses to my parents for next to nothing. God's provision my father said. He said that about me too." She smiled again. "He said I was the most precious homeless person they ever took in."

Gage smiled with her. "They never had any of their own?"

"My mother had two miscarriages. Then the doctors told her she would never conceive. They decided to make Hope their child, but then I came along and my mother said she had to have me, so even though they were in their fifties they adopted me."

"Have you ever looked for your natural parents?"

Raine shook her head. "I knew the parents that mattered." She reached up and straightened a picture that had fallen sideways. "Honestly, it never bothered me that I was adopted. I got so much love from the Stills. I never cared about my other parents."

He nodded.

She crossed her arms over her chest. "So, I don't know what it's like to be one of the Jordan Clan, but I did have a good life with my little family. The people that came and went here made it special too."

Gage believed her and it made him happy for her. "Sometimes a replacement family is better than the people who birthed you. Especially when they're in a bad place."

"Which my birth parents probably were," she added.

They went up the stairs and inspected a few rooms and then came back down. Just as they entered the great room again, the front door creaked. A small woman who looked to be a hundred years old walked in.

Raine recognized her. "Mrs. Belk." She walked over and gave the woman a big hug.

"I was hoping that was you. I saw that funny little car you drive, but I wasn't sure about that Army tank behind it." She raised her head and looked into Gage's eyes.

"Gage Jordan, this is Mrs. Belk. She lives next door and has lived next door for nearly forty years."

They exchanged greetings and Mrs. Belk went on, "The city keeps coming over here looking at this place. They done had all kinds of inspections and surveys."

Gage could see the tension in Raine's neck and shoulders.

"You can't let it go, Rainey. You need to open this place back up."

Raine shook her head. "Mrs. Belk, I don't have the money or…" her voice trailed off.

"Or the will," Mrs. Belk said finishing her thought. "Baby, your parents ran this place for thirty years. For thirty years they helped people get their lives back together."

Raine shook her head. "That was their dream. Their passion. It's not mine." Even Gage could recognize that wasn't true. Raine continued. "This would be too much for me. I work full time."

"So you get other people to help you. You get some of that grant money the go'ment always giving away and hire somebody."

"My parents worked here full-time and it was hardly ever enough." Raine continued her protest, but Gage could see it was falling on death ears.

"You find volunteers. You're educated, baby. You know how to put stuff like that together. Ya folks didn't do that much of that. They liked doing everything themselves, but it's a new day and places like this can be done different than the old way."

Raine's eyes filled with tears again. Gage could tell that this conversation was tearing her apart.

"You don't give up hope," Mrs. Belk pressed. "This place means something in this community. Everybody misses the sunshine that it brought us. It was our hope."

Raine shook her head. "Excuse me," she said and she flew out the door.

Mrs. Belk looked up at him. Her hundred year old eyes were sad. "She just scared. I don't know who you are to her, but please help her. This here is her legacy. This is all she got left of 'dem." Mrs. Belk reached into her pocket. "I have a couple of extra sets of keys. I know she has a set, but maybe you can take these and give them to her. She might need them for a workman." She handed them to him. "I'm gonna pray she hires one."

Gage accepted the keys.

Mrs. Belk made one final plea. "Please talk to her."

Gage nodded. "I'll try." He looked at the picture of the scripture from Isaiah and said, "I should take that for her."

"Taking it down would mean we've given up hope. Let's wait," Mrs. Belk said. He followed her out the door and locked it behind him. He looked around for Raine. He was glad she hadn't gotten in her car and driven away.

"You'll find her in the backyard. She spent her entire childhood back there," Mrs. Belk said.

"I'll have her stop in before we leave."

"No need. I got a feeling 'bout you. She gon' be back." Mrs. Belk smiled and with more speed than anyone her age should have, she hurried back to her house next door.

Gage followed the cement walkway to the rear of the house and found Raine sitting on a swing set. She looked worn out. She'd gotten to a good place in her spirit about visiting the house when she'd been sharing memories with him, but then the thought of keeping Hope House drained all her joy.

"You okay?" he asked, making his approach.

She shrugged. "I'm fine. I just want to make my peace without the burden of public opinion."

He nodded. "That's your right. I'm sure Mrs. Belk just cares about you and your family's legacy."

"She's had to endure the vagrants and that's not fair to her. There's a big difference between a facility that's being managed and vacant houses that the homeless are squatting in."

He nodded again. "Of course. I don't want to add to the voices in your head telling you what to do, but maybe you can just keep it until you decide whether you want to open it again. That part isn't a rush is it?"

An annoyed expression came over her face. "At this point, I'd have to fight for it. I've missed some deadlines with the city."

Gage heard a noise. A rustling sound. He raised a finger to shush her. "Go back to the car." He turned in the direction of the noise he'd heard.

He walked toward the rear porch. As he got closer, he could see a man lying on the floor of the adjacent screened porch. He was wearing Army issued clothing.

"Hey, what are you doing in there soldier?"

The man sat up. Then he stood and saluted Gage.

"What's your name, solider?" Gage asked.

"Corporal Adam Lane, sir."

"At ease, soldier" Gage said.

The young man relaxed.

76

Gage took in his uniform. It was filthy. The knees were torn out of the pants. He'd been resting his head on an Army issued backpack that probably held the rest of his clothes. "How did you know who I was?"

"I read about you in the paper, sir."

He looked back at Raine who had not heeded his instruction to go the car.

"Can I have a minute?" he asked her.

She nodded like she understood. He was sure she probably did. She had seen her father working with Vets over the years and without a doubt she had witnessed the respect brothers gave to each other. Once she was gone he asked, "What are you doing here, Corporal Lane?"

"Sir, I'm between jobs. I'm trying to get some things together."

Gage sighed grievously. "What happened to your housing?"

"I was living with my wife. She asked me to leave, sir."

"Why?" Gage pressed.

"It was scary for her, sir." The pregnant pause that filled the air was almost audible. Then the soldier said, "I'm getting some help at the V.A., sir." He proceeded to tell Gage about his experiences with the V.A. The counseling was good, but there wasn't any help with the real problem. Housing. When the young man finished, Gage reached into his pocket for his wallet and removed some cash. "You know the restaurant down the street? I want you to go have dinner there."

The young man looked at the money like he'd never seen cash before. Gage knew then that he truly was hungry. "Do you have a bus pass?"

Corporal Lane nodded. "Yes, sir."

"Take the bus down to the Davidson Street shelter.

There will be a bed there for you. Give them my name if anyone questions it. My cousin, Kay Jordan, operates the place. I'll make the arrangements."

He nodded again. Raised his hand to salute Gage and said through teary eyes. "Thank you, sir." Then he turned and walked out of the backyard.

Gage looked up toward heaven and asked, "God, why is it like this? Why do so many of my brothers serve and come back to nothing?"

He'd asked this question a thousand times and gotten no answers. He hated the silence. It broke his heart that he couldn't do anything about it.

"He was crying." Raine's voice came from behind him. He turned. His own eyes were wet with disappointment.

"There's a lot to cry about," Gage replied picking up a few empty cans and bottles and putting them in a trash can. "Your father's work was important. That's why he keeps coming back here. There was hope here."

Raine expelled a breath. "There isn't anymore." She turned and left him standing in the backyard wondering why she'd given up on not only this ministry, but also on herself.

Chapter 9

Gage entered the house through the backdoor. He walked in on a conversation between his sisters and because they tended to be quite entertaining he decided to stop and listen.

"You have got to stop being so picky," Brooke said.

"I am not picky. I'm just particular about who I want to spend the rest of my life with," Cree replied.

"You had two marriage proposals last year and you turned down both of them."

"Don't play. You know Richard was wrong for wearing that too little suit to church." Cree rolled her eyes. "Plus, he was short. I was never going to get used to his height."

"What was wrong with Craig?"

Cree shivered. "Girl, he let his fingernails grow too long. It was weird."

Now, Arielle and Brooke rolled their eyes.

"And he didn't have any money. I need my man to have a little coin stashed up. He should have been a doctor and a lawyer with all that student loan debt."

Arielle raised an eyebrow. "You didn't tell us about that."

"See, that's what I mean. You need to know I'm not being picky. I'm being selective. I need a man with the four C's."

Arielle frowned. "What are the four C's?"

Brooke replied, "Color, cut, clarity and carat weight."

Cree shook her head rapidly. "A woman with all four would know."

Brooke raised her hand and smiled at her ring finger. "Of course I am, because Marcus knows what to do."

"I'm not talking about the four C's in a ring," Cree continued.

Brooke smirked. "Then you need to explain."

"I'm talking about the four Cree Jordan four that come before the diamond. Cute, cash, credit, centimeters."

"Centimeters?" Arielle cocked her head. "I'm scared to know where you're going with that."

Gage was curious himself. He was terrified at what he was about to learn.

"Get your mind out of the gutter. Centimeters as in height. No short men. I need to be able to look up at my man." Cree pouted. "Anyway, once I get the first four C's, then he can go get the other four."

Brooke sighed. "You are a mess. You and your four C's are going to get old together."

"Says the person who is engaged to Marcus Thompson. Tall, dark, handsome, fine, rich, well-spoken, and whatever else a sistah has on her list. I can't even go on without hatin' on you."

The oven dinged. Brooke turned it off and donned mitts. "Set your heart on finding the man God has for you. God knows what you need more than you do," she said removing a pan of brownies.

Cree moaned, "Girl, God is not going to do anything for me that I can do for myself. I can screen out the duds."

On that note, Gage made his presence known. "I just learned more in the past three minutes than I've learned in my entire career in the military."

Arielle and Brooke laughed.

Cree continued to pout. "Gage, help me out. Do you think being picky is a bad thing?"

Gage raised a hand to his sister's back and rubbed in reassuring circles. "There's nothing wrong with being picky. You be picky until Jesus comes back and when He gets here you can marry Him."

Cree squinted and hit him playfully on the arm. "Lot of help you are. Not like you're ever serious about anybody."

Brooke leaned on the island and removed the oven mitts. "We don't actually know if Gagey here has been serious about anyone because he can hide them."

Arielle nodded. "True. He could already have a wife. Someone that he doesn't want to introduce to the family."

Brooke turned up her nose. "You mean like a white woman?"

Cree leaned over the counter. "No, she means like Savant." The women giggled.

Arielle laughed too, but then shushed her sisters. "You know Cade has supersonic hearing."

"Well, I wish his vision was just as good. He might have seen that thang coming." Cree's lips twisted into an exaggerated frown.

The laughter stopped. They all sighed heavily and then Brooke said, "We need to be praying. Trash talking Savant is not going to fix a thing."

"And Cade isn't perfect. Trust me. I shared a room with him when we were kids," Gage said, tossing an apple up and down before taking a bite.

Arielle poked him in the side. "Back to you, Officer Jordan and your story on the women."

"I've been deployed too many times to keep a woman."

"Don't front. Soldiers get cuffed all the time," Cree said. "Especially good looking ones like you."

Gage shrugged. "Sometimes you don't want to bring someone else into your misery."

"Well, you're out now," Arielle teased, "and your old behind is getting close to forty. You don't want to have kids in your sixties."

"Speaking of old parents," Cree interjected, smiling. "You seemed to be in hero mode last night with Raine Still."

Gage couldn't keep back the smile that crept over his face. "A woman with a dead battery is not hero mode. That's just being a man."

"Uh, huh, except that the two of you were locking eyes at the ticket booth before that battery went dead," Cree pressed.

"I agree," Arielle teased. "You two could have held hands and touched that car and got the battery charged."

The women laughed in unison.

"You did disappear from the show," Brooke continued.

"And then you were you late for church this morning!" Cree shrieked.

The Jordan sisters laughed out loud again. They were enjoying themselves way too much.

"What gives?" Cree asked. "You're never late for anything."

"If you nosy women must know, I took her back to her car this morning and charged the battery."

"Where does she live," Brooke asked, raising a knife to the brownies and slicing them into squares.

"Not too far from Southpark mall," he replied.

Cree snatched her head back. "So, let me get this straight. You left home, went south to Southpark and then went all the way back up to the Plaza before church?"

"I get up at five," Gage said to be clear.

"And I'm sure she appreciated the help," Evelyn Jordan said walking into the kitchen. "It's always good to know you raised your children right." She kissed Gage on the cheek. "Your father told me to tell you tip off is in three minutes."

"Kick off, Mother," Cree corrected.

Their mother waved a dismissive hand. "Kick off, tick off...the game is starting."

Gage laughed. "I am glad to escape this group."

"Her name ends in an 'e'. She'll fit right in the family," Arielle teased.

"Uh, huh," Cree's voice sounded behind him. "Gage and Raine sitting in a tree. K-i-s-s-i-n-g."

Kissing Raine. Cree had no idea how accurate she had been about what he'd wanted last night. And while he felt good about not taking things too far with her, he regretted that he hadn't gotten that kiss. It had been a long time since he'd kissed a woman. A long time since he'd even had a date. A month in the hospital, five months in rehab, and then the months of counseling and such after were not an attractive time.

The one woman he had been chatting with a bit prior to his last deployment had moved on. It was for the best. He wasn't going to marry her anyway. He wasn't going to marry anyone it seemed. He was always moving. He didn't know how to bring someone into that situation, so he hadn't. He'd been dismissing that notion since that day he'd spent with Raine years ago. That unplanned date had been the first time he'd wondered to himself, "What if?" "Would it be a crime to get involved with someone?" The answer he'd convinced himself of was "yes", so he put the flashes of her smile, her laughter, her scent and everything else about her that kept creeping into his memory from his mind and got on the plane to Iraq without a second thought. He returned to war without her address or phone number, but not without regret.

He entered the home theater room and claimed a seat amongst his father and brothers, Cade and Drake. Chase was catering an event so he was missing their Sunday ritual.

Drake stood and walked over to the buffet table his mother had set up in the corner. He picked up a beer, twisted off the top and with pure devilment in his tone, sang, "How 'bout dem Cowboys?"

Gage, their father and Cade gave him the evil eyes. The Jordan's were Panther fans and once the Panthers were out of the game, they were rooting for the Seattle. But somehow, Drake had gone off to Southern Methodist University, fallen in love with Olivia, a Dallas Cowboys cheerleader, and married her. Her allegiance was always with the Cowboys and now so was his. The two had only recently relocated back to Charlotte and brought their Cowboys fanaticism and memorabilia with them.

"You know you 'bout to get hurt in here," Cade threatened.

"No, my team is about to win," Drake replied reaching for a plate and some wings. He danced around like the show-off he was and then plopped down in a chair next to Cade.

Cade reached toward him and took his plate away. "You should have brought your own chicken if you wasn't gonna be rooting for the right team."

Their father intervened, "No, let him eat. He can't get sick if he loses on an empty stomach."

Gage shook his head at the back and forth banter between his brothers. The doorbell rang and minutes later three of his first cousins entered the room. Troy, Kevin and Henry Jordan II were all his father's brother's children. Each Sunday during the playoffs the Jordan men got to together after church for the game. They rotated houses and responsibility for the brew and the snacks. The men pounded fists and filled in the empty seats.

"Y'all are just in time," Cade said, moving a bowl of chips off the empty seat next to him. "Where's Uncle H?"

Uncle H was Henry Jordan, Senior. His dad's older brother and a closeted Cowboys fan also.

"He had a delivery," Troy said, referring to his father's career as an obstetrician. "Can you believe that? What kind of kid is born at kick off during the playoffs?"

The men laughed and their father said, "It's got to be a girl. No respect for timing."

"No doubt," Cade added. "Only a woman would be that annoying."

Everyone looked at him and Gage knew the same thing was on their mind that was on his. Cade's sour grapes with Savant were squished and leaking.

"There's the kick!" Drake yelled, pulling everyone's attention to the big screen. The watching of the game began.

Gage remembered how they watched the games overseas. They could sometimes catch them on base, but not once they were in a combat zone, which was where they spent the majority of their tour. Sports were the great equalizer. There were a lot of hard days in deployment, but when they could enjoy a game back on base together, it was all good.

Gage's best friend, J.J. worshiped the game. With J.J.'s death, watching football had become less entertaining because of the memories. The ear-splitting bang of explosives sounded to his memory. Gage closed his eyes and went back to the day that changed his life.

Gage heard the sound again. That gurgle that he imagined was blood bubbling and moving through holes in places that weren't supposed to have holes. The sound was so loud it was deafening. He never would have thought you could hear blood.

He forced himself to run faster. The pain in his leg was so bad he thought it would give out on him. He decided it would have to, because he couldn't stop. His breaths came harder. He looked down at J.J. His eyes were closed. If it weren't for the fact that he was carrying him, he would have thought he was just sleeping. If it weren't for that gurgle, he'd be afraid he was dead. But a dead man's blood didn't make sounds. It didn't move. Only pumping blood could do that, so there was hope.

Gage wasn't crazy. He knew he was losing him. He had to make J.J. fight. He had to get him to open his eyes. He wouldn't die if he was looking at him. Would he?

"Coach me, J.J.!" Gage yelled.

J.J.'s eyes fluttered and opened.

"Coach me through the play." Gage slowed for a second, adjusted the 180 pound man in his arms and took off running again. He felt something pop in his knee. The pain caused him to stumble a little, but he kept pushing.

"Second down," J.J. whispered. "This is it. You got the ball and you need to make sure he don't…" Coughing. This time blood gushed from his mouth and nose.

Hot tears ran down Gage's face. He stole a glance at J.J. His eyes were closed again.

"Make sure he don't what?" Gage cried. He looked ahead. He could see the medi-vac copter through the trees. Less than half a mile.

He could do it. He could make it less than a mile. J.J. coughed. Gage heard that sound again. The gurgle.

"Jay," he yelled crying. "They got the ball. Tell me what to do!"

J.J. opened his eyes again. "Catch that running back!"

A roar rushed through the room. "Running back!" Drake yelled, jumping to his feet. "One, two, three, dodge all them suckers!" And then seconds later, "Touchdown! Yeah boy! Whew! We ain't even fifteen minutes into this game and 'dem Cowboys done scored!"

All the other Jordan's rolled their eyes and reached for drinks, chicken or chips.

"I told you. I'm so glad some of you suckers put money on this game. You can't stop 'em," Drake sang.

"Drake," his father raised his voice like he was talking to an annoying little boy.

Everyone in the room looked at Nathaniel Jordan to see what was next. Drake was too old to spank. Drake raised an eyebrow.

"Ya mama called you. Go see what she wants."

As the baby boy of the family, Drake had a special relationship with his mother. When she called, he ran. Just like they knew he would. The dancing and celebrating stopped instantly. Drake rushed from the home theater room.

Cade shook his head. "I didn't hear anything."

"She didn't call him," his father said. "Somebody lock that door. Maybe he'll go home."

Cade popped to his feet, closed the door and turned the lock. "Squirrely rascal will probably come through the heat vent."

The men laughed and talked about the disappointing play while they ate.

"So, Gage, you ready for your interview?" Troy asked, turning his attention to him.

"What interview?" Kevin asked with interest. Kevin was a head hunter for a major employment firm. He'd been trying to get Gage to sign on with him since he'd come home. Gage had declined, not wanting to involve his cousin in what might be a wishy-washy effort on his part. He had no idea what he really wanted to do and he had no intentions on accepting an employment contract if he really didn't want the job. It was easier to be flaky with strangers than family.

Flaky. That's a word that had never in the history of his life been associated with him, but he was starting to feel that way.

"It's Homeland Security," Troy offered like it was his news to share. Troy was a lawyer and a pretty successful one. Gage always wondered how he managed to keep all his client's secrets, but didn't seem to be able to keep anyone else's. "I heard it was a big shot spot too," Troy continued. "Nice piece of change, lots of travel, and a pretty well funded department."

Gage leaned back in his chair. That was a bit much, even for Troy. He'd barely talked about the position to anyone. Partly because he hadn't wanted to jinx himself and partly because there again, he wasn't sure he wanted to take it if they offered it to him. "And how do you know so much?"

"Charlotte is still small and the director is one of our clients. I ran into him at your award ceremony. When he asked why I was there, I told him we were one in the same Jordan."

Gage nodded understanding. The local director of Homeland was indeed at his ceremony, as were all the big shots in town with the Vice President in attendance.

Troy continued, "He asked me lots of questions about you. The job is yours. They like the idea of having a distinguished veteran such as yourself on their payroll."

Gage nodded again. Troy was right. It was a great job, for the right person.

He'd spent all those months in rehab, thinking and contemplating what he would do if he had to leave the Army and then months after trying to fool the doctors into thinking he was recovering when he knew he wasn't. He told himself he was hoping for a miracle and waiting on God to deliver it. But in truth, Gage knew that he'd already heard from God. After he woke up from surgery, he knew things had changed for him. He'd sustained too much damage to his leg. The running after the injury had shred his tendon from the middle of the thigh to the middle of the calf and his knee was messed up too.

There was a knock on the door and then Drake's voice on the other side. "Come on y'all. Don't be like that. It's not about who wins, it's how you play the game."

The Jordan men all looked at each other and simultaneously said, "Nah."

Drake knocked again. "Come on. All the Buffalo wings are in there. My car keys are in there."

They continued to laugh about leaving Drake out in hallway and then Gage stood and let his younger brother in.

"Thanks. An officer and a gentleman." Drake saluted him strolling back to his seat.

"Just behave yourself," Gage warned. He made his way to the buffet table and picked up some food.

Cade joined him at the buffet table. "Speaking of being a gentleman. Tell us about what happened with Raine last night."

Gage did not like all this attention his simple goodwill gesture toward Raine was stirring up.

"Raine who," know-it-all Troy asked, hunting gossip.

"Raine Still," Cade offered. "You probably don't know her. She went to school with us."

"I know Raine Still," Troy replied.

Now Gage was interested in Troy's ramblings. His cousin was not only an expert at handling law cases, but he was also good at running through pretty women.

"Our firm handled the business for her parents some years back. We do a lot of pro-bono work and I was involved in one of the cases. Anyway, Raine would always come in and help her parents with stuff," Troy said. Then he added, "Are you dating her? She's a quiet one, but still a fox."

Gage smiled inwardly. That she was. "No, we're not dating. I helped her with some car trouble."

"Car trouble." Troy smiled slyly. "Right." Then his face took on a serious expression. "Really sad about her parents though. Real sad about everything going on with Hope House."

"Whoa! Interception!" Drake yelled. He jumped up and did a sideline dance.

Everyone's attention was on the screen except Gage. He waited for things to quiet down from the play and then got Troy's attention again. "What do you mean about Hope House?"

Troy raised a beer and took a long swig. "It's being condemned. Once they knock it down, the city is going to sell the land. The rumor is a liquor store chain is waiting to buy it."

"Are you sure? I was over there today. It needs some

work, but it doesn't look like it's condemnable."

Troy shrugged. "I'm just telling you what I know. I'm surprised Raine isn't trying to fight it. She only has a few days before the city takes ownership."

Gage mumbled to himself. "I think all the fight's gone out of her."

Troy raised an eyebrow. "What was that?"

Gage shook his head. "Nothing important. Thanks for telling me about the city."

Troy shrugged. "No problem."

The game ended. The cousins left. Cade, Drake, his father and himself were the only ones left in the room.

Gage had been thinking about Hope House since Troy shared the story about the city and now he knew he couldn't dismiss the nagging feeling in his gut. "I need a favor."

The trio looked at each other and then at him. Gage was not one who asked for favors. He didn't ask for anything, not even when he was a kid. "I need you guys to go to Hope House with me."

Chapter 10

The ride to Hope House was quicker than Gage thought it would be. A straight shot down I-77, a few turns and they were there. The men rolled out of the vehicle. Their father led the approach to the house. Like they already knew their assignments, Cade and Drake went around back. Gage let his father in the front door with the key he'd gotten from Mrs. Belk.

"It's brick," his father said. "That's always a good sign. The outside structure looks sound." They stepped into the dark house and a blast of freezing cold air hit them. The arid, musty smell did too. A big mouse or small rat scurried across the floor. His father turned, looked at him and asked, "What are you getting yourself involved in, son?"

Gage shook his head. "I don't know."

Nathaniel Jordan nodded and continued to walk through every room in the house. Before long, Cade and Drake came in using powerful keychain flashlights like the one his father had.

"Not too bad," Drake said. "The neighborhood itself is much worse than the house. I think we woke half the homeless population in Charlotte in that other house."

Gage raised an eyebrow. "How'd you get in?"

Drake kicked at the baseboards. "This is some good wood," he said and then he answered Gage's question. "The backdoor is hanging off the hinges."

"Drugs?" their father asked.

Cade shook his head. "No, just a bunch of men with no where to go."

Vets, Gage thought. He sighed heavily and raked his hand over his hair. He hated this. He hated the thought of men he had served alongside of living in abandoned buildings. It wasn't right. They needed help. "What does it need?" he asked.

"We have to do a thorough inspection," his father stated. "We need light and our equipment."

"Can you give me an estimate on how much money?" Gage asked. He had some money saved from his years in the military, but it was not in great supply. The idea of a loan was laughable. He didn't have a job.

Cade was the money man of the group, so he answered, "It's hard to tell. We've got to take a look at plumbing and electrical. Those are big items. We'll get a generator in here and let you know."

"Are you thinking about buying it?" Drake interjected, frowning.

Gage looked at the sign with the scripture engraved on it. Raine's father's reminder of hope from Isaiah. "I'm thinking about Raine. She's connected to this place, but she doesn't know where to start. If I can help her figure out her options then she can make an informed decision," Gage said. He closed the distance between himself and his father with a few steps. "This is kind of a rush thing. How soon can you check it out?"

His father put a hand on his shoulder. "For you son, we can do it first thing in the morning." He smiled and Gage smiled a little too. The smile was the start of something he hadn't felt in a long time. *Hope.*

Chapter 11

"So, spill," Kiara said. "What were you doing with that Gage guy and how long have you been doing it?"

Raine stared back at her best friend's image on her iPad. She paused. What was she doing with Gage? Nothing at this point. "I'm not doing anything with him. I went to The Show Saturday."

"The Show? I thought you couldn't get a ticket."

"I couldn't, but it turns out they held some for me. In my mother's honor. Isn't that sweet?"

"Very," Kiara replied.

Raine watched as her friend dipped her finger into a jar of hair custard, spread it along the length of her shoulder length natural hair and began to plait. "You're going to be doing your hair for hours. It's so thick."

"Who are you telling? At least it'll be done before Rick gets home," Kiara said, referring to her new husband. "He always offers to help me and he has two left thumbs. He makes such a mess."

"I wish I had thick hair like that."

"And I wish I had that nice straight hair you have on your head," Kiara remarked with more than a little agitation in her voice. "Now, stop changing the subject. Tell me about Gage."

"Okay, so when I came out of the theater my car wouldn't start. He tried to help me. Waited for the auto club that never came with me and then this morning he came and charged the battery."

"Oh," Kiara's disappointment was evident. "That was sweet of him to come back this morning."

"Very."

"So, when was he following you?"

"After he fixed the car. He followed me to Hope House."

"Why?"

"I don't know."

Kiara stopped twisting her hair on that point. "Excuse me? What do you mean you don't know?"

"I didn't ask him. I was caught up in my emotions. I just…I didn't ask him why he was there."

"Does he live in the neighborhood?"

"No, he lives in Myers Park."

Kiara snatched her head back. "Myers Park, eh. So, he drove from Myers Park to Southpark to the theater and then followed you to the hood?"

"Yes."

"Hmmm…" Kiara affected a bored look, although, Raine could see the gleam in her eye.

"Hmmm what?"

"That's a lot of driving to be nice."
Raine agreed, but she also knew he had good home training. "He's a nice guy."

"Where has Mr. Nice Guy been in all these years? You never mentioned him."

"Remember, I told you he was in the Army. He's been

overseas."

Kiara confirmed understanding with a nod of her head. "Right, he was being deployed when you two went out before."

"Well, we didn't really go out."

"You hung out, for hours. It might have been an impromptu date, but it was a date all the same."

Raine shrugged. "Then he left."

"But he's back and being nice." Kiara smiled. "Is he married?"

"He says no."

"Gay?" Kiara frowned.

"I don't know. I hope not."

"What do you mean you hope not? Has he done something to make you think he is?"

Raine thought about the kiss she didn't get last night. His excuse for why he hadn't. She'd dismissed it, thinking maybe he wasn't attracted to her, but there might be more. Could he be gay? "Oh God, I can't even imagine that. He's so perfect."

Kiara let out an exasperated breath. "Down low men usually are."

"It doesn't matter. I don't really expect to see him again," Raine lied, hoping that wasn't possible.

Her cell phone rang. Raine looked at the name she'd saved with the number. She shrieked, "Kiara, it's him."

"He's going to live a long time. That's what my grandma always said when you talked somebody up."

Raine swiped the screen and said, "Hi, Gage."

"Hey to you." She could hear a smile in his voice.

"Look, I was calling because I was wondering if you'd like to go out with me. On a date."

"A date?" she said the phrase like he was speaking Chinese.

"I'd like to see you again."

Raine smiled and stuttered over her words. "I…I don't see any reason why not."

"Good." He sounded relieved. "How about Tuesday evening?"

Raine felt excitement surge in her chest. "Like the day after tomorrow?"

"Yes, there's someplace I'd like to go and Tuesday would be a good night."

"Sure, Tuesday is fine," she said bobbing her head like he could see her.

"Great. Can we plan on six?" he asked.

Raine nodded like he could see her through the phone. "Sure, six is good."

"Great. I look forward to seeing you again. I'll be at your door at six sharp."

Raine ended the call and looked at Kiara. "He asked me out."

"I heard," she teased.

"I can't believe he wants to go out with me. I guess he's not gay."

Kiara curled her lip. "You can still ask him."

"I can't ask him that. Why would he ask me out if he was?"

"Girl, don't get me to telling why. It would go over your head. Ask him or don't ask him, but if he's not, please just try to have a good time. Get to know him and let him get to know you."

"Get to know me." Raine chuckled joylessly. "He'll be bored to tears."

"Raine, you're my best friend. If you're boring what does that say about me?"

"That you're generous," Raine laughed. "I need to turn in. I have some thinking and praying to do."

"Call me Wednesday and let me know how it goes on the date."

"I will."

"And Raine," she paused for effect, "please don't give up Hope."

Raine nodded. "That's what I need to pray about."

"Okay, girl, love you."

Raine's heart smiled. "Love you more."

They ended the video chat.

Raine sat back in the chair. She closed the iPad case and slid it away from her.

A date. Her first actual man picking her up at her door date since prom and that wasn't even really a date. He was the son of a volunteer at Hope. Taking her to prom had been community service for him. But this was a real date with a man who was really interested in her. She'd have to figure out a great outfit.

Her phone beeped in a text message. She picked it up and was excited to see it was from Gage.

Wear jeans and a tee shirt on Tuesday. Let me know if you have any food allergies.

Jeans and a tee shirt. Raine was just getting swept away

by the idea of something fancy. She shrugged it off. She'd put on a potato sack to spend time with him. She texted him back that she had no allergies.

Then she stood and went from room to room turning off the lights. When she reached her sitting room/office, she paused and looked at the pills and the glass of water she'd been prepared to wash them down with. Raine knew she should throw the pills away, but she was tired and decided tomorrow would do. She cut off the light and climbed the stairs towards her bedroom. Even if it was just jeans, she had another outfit to pick out.

Chapter 12

Freedom Park was his favorite place to watch the sun rise. Gage sat on the hood of his truck many mornings doing just that. It was 5:50 a.m. He'd been awake for over an hour already. He couldn't lie in his bed, or even stay in the house anymore. The Army had ruined him. He'd been waking up at five for most of his adult life.

Gage climbed down from the truck, stretched for a few minutes and began the painful process of trying to run. He'd gone less than two miles and had to stop. He dropped to the ground and put his head in his hands. He hated this. He hated his injury. He hated the pain. He hated that he couldn't run fifteen miles anymore. But more than anything, he hated that it bothered him so much, because the same shrapnel that had injured him had killed J.J. His frustration left him feeling ungrateful. But the longer he sat there, the more he knew that this morning's failure was not about running. It wasn't even about J.J. Today, he needed answers.

"God show me. Tell me. What am I supposed to do?" he asked.

What he wanted to do didn't make sense. He wanted to walk away from the big federal job that was waiting for him. He wanted to counsel vets for what would amount to thankless pay. He'd get by with his military disability payment, but walking away from a six figure salary seemed insane. Still, he wanted to save Hope House, no matter what it took, even if it took every dime he had saved. He wanted Raine Still. A woman he barely knew. A woman who wasn't even sure if she wanted herself. The funny thing to him was that Raine was the easiest of his decisions when in truth she should have been the most complex. Gage knew he wanted Raine from the moment their eyes locked at the theater. When he looked into her eyes he saw possibilities. He saw his future. He saw his wife.

"Are you okay, buddy?" Another runner slowed his pace to ask.

"I'm good," Gage replied. "Bad knee."

"Sorry to hear that. An elliptical keeps my wife in shape," the guy said as he sprinted off.

Gage appreciated the advice, but runners knew there was no substitute for running. Running wasn't just about staying in shape. It was a way to clear the mind, renew the soul. He missed not being able to do that. Two miles simply was not enough time to get his head together.

He pushed himself off the ground and walked back to his truck. He climbed in, closed the door and threw his head back against the headrest. He was still thinking about Raine. He could not escape her. Gage wasn't sure he was supposed to.

"I knew your mother was the only woman in the world for me," his father said. Gage had been ten the first time he heard this story. It was an anniversary dinner. The dinners were much simpler twenty-six years ago when Nathaniel Jordan was building Jordan Home Renovations and trying to raise seven kids on one income. Though the celebration was unembellished, the story never changed. "I knew your mother was going to be my wife the first time I laid eyes on her. That's why I proposed two days later. It took her four more days to say yes and then we were married three days later."

Gage had convinced himself that day, at ten that he would be like his father. He would know his wife when he saw her. And so it went for the last twenty-six years. He'd met a lot of women. Dated more then he could even remember. But no one looked like forever to him until Raine and if he was honest with himself, she looked like forever in high school and at the wedding and on that impromptu date. He just hadn't been ready to process it then.

His parents had forty years of love and devotion after ten days of knowing each other. Was that even possible in today's time? He turned the key in the ignition and pulled the car away from the curb. Gage had a feeling he was going to find out.

It was early enough for him to miss rush hour traffic. He stopped for coffee and made the trip to Hope House. When he arrived, he was surprised to see the house lit up and even more surprised to see Cade's truck parked out front. A large generator sat in the walkway with a long cord that Gage assumed ran to the main power line for the house. He hopped out and went inside.

"Cade," he called. "It's me, Gage."

A minute later, Cade came walking down the stairs. "I'm glad you still know how to not get yourself shot."

"Yeah, yeah, you're all talk." Gage chuckled. "I do hope you actually have a weapon since you up here in this hood before sunup."

"I've been in this business too long not to be strapped," Cade replied, "but thankfully, the good Lord has my back. I've never had to pull it out."

Gage removed the lid from his coffee cup and took a long sip. "Care to tell me why I'm finding you here this early?"

Cade raised an eyebrow. "Sometimes work is the best medicine for what ails you."

"And you need to take it at the crack of dawn?"

"If there was a bed in this joint and some heat I would have slept here last night." Cade groaned and then said, "Let me change that. It was cold in my house, so I don't need the heat."

Gage shook his head. "Man, what's going on with you and Savant?"

Cade hooked a finger through the toolkit on his waist. He paused for a long time before answering with a shake of his head. "I don't know."

Gage drank more coffee. "Have you guys tried some counseling?"

"She won't go."

"Does she recognize something's wrong?"

"Savant recognizes there's something wrong with me." He chuckled painfully. "That's the only thing she sees as wrong."

"What about the kids?"

Cade shook his head. "I'm trying, but I can't save them from this. Not by myself. She's got to try. I don't know how much longer she'll stay."

Gage sighed long and hard.

"Just be glad you're not married. It's not like it was for mom and dad. These women are different."

"Don't bring all women into it. Chase and Pamela?" Gage said, referring to his older brother and his wife. They had been married for over fifteen years and still appeared to be on a honeymoon.

"Rare," Cade quipped.

"Drake and Olivia?"

"Practically newlyweds."

Gage shook his head at his brother's cynicism. "Can I do anything to help?"

"I need a miracle. Keep us in prayer."

Gage nodded. "I can do that." A few minutes of silence filled the room with Gage finishing his coffee and Cade going through paperwork on a clipboard.

"So, speaking of miracles," Cade said.

Gage steeled himself for the bad news. "This place doesn't need one. I'm not really sure what's going on with the city inspector's recommendation. I'll have to send someone over there to get the report so I can see what they found. But in the meantime, Drake and I were in agreement yesterday. Both houses need roofs, but this one could be patched to hold out a little longer. That burned out room needs to be cleaned up. Both need quite a few windows, some flooring, paint, an exterminator and a good cleaning. Not anywhere near condemnable."

Gage was speechless. "What kind of money are we talking about to get it open?"

Cade shrugged. "I'd say less than twenty grand if you patch this roof instead of replace it."

"If we use local labor?"

Cade squinted. "Local as in…what do you mean local?"

"A few folks from the neighborhood and all Jordan hands on deck for a weekend?"

Cade sighed. "Well it's pretty obvious I need to get out of the house, so you got me. If you can get the rest of those folks to give you a day of hard work, I'd say we're closer to fifteen grand. Most of it would be the roofs and the windows."

"That's not bad."

"Yeah, but then there's the taxes and the mortgage if it has one."

"Raine and I will work that out."

Cade squinted. "Raine and you as in you and her?"

Gage looked at his brother over his coffee cup. He knew his silence told Cade what he wanted to know, because his response was rapid fire.

"Please tell me you are not going to do this thing with that woman. You don't even know her. You met her two days ago. Not even two days. A night and an half ago."

"I've known her longer than that. It's complicated."

Cade shook his head wildly. "No brother, not complicated. It's crazy."

Gage let out a long sigh. "It's hard to explain."

"Gage, I don't mind helping her with this situation. But tell me how in the world you have even set your mind to think you should be investing in this place with her? You have a good job lined up."

"I'm not going to take that job."

Cade shrugged. "Then join us at Jordan Homes."

Gage shook his head. "That's not what I'm supposed to be doing."

"What do you know about transitional housing and group homes?"

"Nothing. But I know vets and I know this place used to be one that they could count on for a good night's sleep, a meal and some conversation."

"I understand what you want to do, but aren't most of those homeless guys mentally ill?"

Gage bit down on his lip, quelling his temper before speaking. He didn't want to lash out at his brother for something he didn't understand. "You think I'm well? The only difference between me and those guys is I had a family to come home to. I went in with more rank because of my education so I was paid more and could save more money. But I'm not different. I have the same nightmares and the same images in my head during the day. I can't turn my back and disappear into a federal building like that's God's plan for my life."

Cade threw up his hands. "Okay, so even if you want to work with vets, why tie yourself to Raine before you know what you're actually tying yourself down to?"

Gage recognized more hurt in his brother's voice. He'd enjoyed a short engagement to Savant and then a rather quickly put together wedding. The pain that consumed Cade was projected onto every word that came out of his mouth about women.

"I trust this," Gage said pointing to his belly. "My gut doesn't steer me wrong. It never has, not in life and not on a combat mission."

His friend J.J. immediately flashed into his mind.

The explosion and then the running. "Hold on, we're almost there."

Gage swallowed and ignored the fact that the memory had shaken his confidence a little. "I trust my heart and I trust what I hear the Spirit telling me in my head."

"And what does she say?"

Gage paused and then stuttered when he spoke. "She doesn't exactly know what I have planned."

Cade laughed. "Well, I think that's her car outside, so you can get that corrected." He leaned over and picked up his tool box. "I have to be at a site in Matthews by eight so I'm going to go. I'll let you know what I find out from the city report later."

"What about this equipment?" Gage asked.

"Drake will be here soon. He handles the electrical

inspections. Just wait for him."

Gage nodded. The brothers pounded fists before Cade opened the door. Raine was standing on the other side of it. Her hair pulled back in a high ponytail. She was wearing sweats and sneakers. Her makeup free face was looking fresh and beautiful. Cade and she exchanged a few words of greeting before his brother left.

She looked like she had no idea what to say. Gage was sure she had initially been shocked to see his and Cade's trucks outside, but she'd had a few minutes to get over that. The look on her face now was puzzlement, pure and simple. "What are you doing here? What was Cade doing here?"

He did a once over. She looked good. Even in sweats. "Jordan's are early risers. That's why we get the worms."

Raine looked at him like he owed her more than platitudes.

Gage knew he did, so he explained. "I asked my father and brothers to take a look at the houses and let me know what was needed to get them up to code. I thought you might want to know so you could make an informed decision."

Raine was noticeably shocked. Gage wasn't sure if it was a good shocked or a bad one. He realized it was her property and he hadn't asked permission.

She cocked an eyebrow. "How did you get in?" Before he could respond she nodded. "Never mind. Mrs. Belk. You're in cahoots with Mrs. Belk."

"She loves you," he replied glad that she wasn't angry.

She stepped in the room and Gage closed the door.

"I'm sorry, Raine. I really shouldn't have done this without you, but I thought if I could tell you what kind of money you were looking at…" He stopped there. This hadn't been just about her. He wanted Hope open and he needed to be honest. He wasn't sure how she'd receive it.

Raine stuck her hands in her pocket and looked down at her sneakers for a moment. When she raised her head he could see wetness in her eyes. Her voice trembled. "This was kind," she said. "I know your father and brothers are busy and for them to take the time to come here…" She paused and shook her head. "I can't get territorial and crazy when your hearts were in the right place. No one else would do this. No one else would take the time or even care."

Gage disagreed and said so, "Lots of people care about what your parents did here. I think there are a lot of people who would help this case."

"Maybe I've gotten cynical."

"You came here first thing this morning because this place is on your heart," he said optimistically. "Don't you have to work today?"

"I telework most days and I don't report until nine. I have time to get back home."

"So, you came here this morning to do what?" Gage asked.

She shrugged like she didn't know.

He believed that. She was like him. Unsure about what to do, but at least for her there was a connection that made sense. For him it was her, she was the only thing that made sense. And then she said why and it didn't make sense to him at all.

"Gage, I appreciate your family's time. I know you'll disagree with my decision, but I think I came to say good-bye."

Chapter 13

Quiet stretched between them. Raine didn't know why Gage looked like she'd sucker punched him, but he did.

"This is too big of a commitment for me," she began. "I'm still paying my mother's medical bills. I need my good paying job."

"You don't like your work."

"That's beside the point."

It was obvious from his expression that Gage did not agree. "No, that's exactly the point."

She parked a hand on her hip. "You must be some kind of romantic, which I find hard to believe with you having been military for so long."

He laughed. "Do you think soldiers don't have feelings and dreams?"

"That's not what I meant."

"You think the war and the suffering knock the hope and fun and touchy feely stuff out of us?"

"I just find it hard to believe a man like you is so... I don't know."

He took a few steps toward her. "So what?" She shook her head. She was like a child refusing to open its mouth and let an adult see what was inside of it. "Raine, so what?"

"So nice and so interested in me and my problems. Tell me why? Are you some kind of altruistic sadist intent on making sure I get myself in over my head? What's this about?"

He shook his head. "Who are you and where is the Raine I said goodbye to yesterday?"

"She did some hard thinking all night and decided this was not her life. Her life didn't have people in it that wanted to help her. Her life didn't have a career doing anything other than working for an insurance company and her life certainly did not have handsome knights in shining armor saving the day."

Gage smiled. "Handsome huh? I hope I have more to offer the world than good genes."

She smirked. "I don't know how to take chances, Gage. I work in risk management."

"Isn't part of risk management about knowing when a risk is a good one?"

She shook her head. "Not in my department."

He paused a beat and said, "I've given it some thought. I don't want to take that federal job. What I actually want to do is work with veterans in a setting like this. I want to use my counseling degree."

She blinked a few times. She could hardly believe her ears. "Are you serious?"

"Yes." He flashed his gleaming smile. Raine was temporarily dazed, but this time it wasn't just his teeth, it was his heart to serve that impressed her.

"You can get a job working with vets anywhere. You could open your own center. Why Hope?"

"Because the community needs it. Why start over somewhere else when what I need is already here? The veterans know this place," he continued. "When I met that soldier yesterday, I knew this was what I needed to do. I just hoped I could convince you."

"This is a lot. It's two houses. You could buy your own and have less overhead."

"People miss Hope. They need it. Besides, if you let it go, it'll be turned into a liquor store. The same guys that are sleeping in the buildings will be buying alcohol here. It's not right. Your parents would hate that."

She winced. He'd sure hit a nerve with that statement.

He continued to plead his case. "I want to stop that. I want to be a part of the solution."

He sounded just like her parents. "My father would love you."

"I'm sure I'd love him, so let's do this. Let's look at the money and figure it out."

She shook her head. "I only have about ten thousand dollars. I've been saving some, but I've been putting everything on paying off my mother's medical debt."

"Ten is half the battle. I've got the other ten."

Raine could hardly believe her ears. "We'd be partners?"

"Yeah, I mean not equal, you own most of it, but I'd be invested. I don't want to take anything away from your family legacy. We can write up my ten as a loan."

More disbelief peppered her tone. "Why would you do that?"

"Because I want to. Why are you questioning me like I'm out of my mind?"

"Because it's crazy," she laughed.

"I know what I'm doing. I'm not a kid. It's not like I've been somewhere with my head in the sand for the past fourteen years. I've been in the desert, but there's nothing like a war to grow you up." He released a long breath. "So, what do you think? No goodbyes, yet?"

Raine walked over to the fireplace and looked up at her father's favorite sign. "I'll think about it," she said, turning back to face him.

"You don't have long."

She sighed. "I know."

He stepped closer, put a hand on her shoulder and said, "This is your parent's legacy. Think about what they would want you to do."

She wanted to think about her parents wishes, but he was too close for her to think about anything other than him. She still wanted that kiss.

Gage removed his hand like he'd read her mind. He wasn't going to kiss her. How had she gone from that almost kiss in his truck to being hooked up with him for Hope House? Was their date really going to be a business meeting? Is that why she was told to wear jeans? Disappointment filled every blood vessel in her body. She wanted love. Companionship. Not a business partner. But like every other time in life she was dependable Raine. Not the Raine a man like Gage would want for anything else.

She needed to protect herself from her emotions. She had to get out of this house and away from this man. "I've got to get home and start working."

He looked at his watch. "It's not even seven. Are you sure we can't have breakfast?"

She wanted to, but she fought saying yes, with a shake of her head. "It's a busy day for me. I have an account that needs a lot of attention."

"What about lunch?" he pressed.

Raine could have screamed for him to stop pushing. Couldn't he see that she was falling for him…had fallen for him years ago? Wasn't it written all over her face? "I can't, but I promise you, I'll think about Hope okay."

She looked around at the space once more. Could she really be here every day without her parents? She wasn't sure she could bear it. Kiara's words ran through her mind. *Make it brand new.*

Gage's voice broke through her thoughts. "Let me walk you out." He swept around her to the door and opened it. They fell into step on the walk to her car. Just as she was about to get in, a van pulled in front of them with the words, Jordan Homes, painted on the door. Drake and another man hopped out.

Gage waved to them and they waved back before pulling equipment out of the rear cargo area.

More Jordans…she was really going to cry now. "Your family is amazing."

"They are," he said, looking back at them for a moment. "They'll become like your family too. Jordans are worse than roaches. You can't get rid of them."

She laughed. "That's good to know in advance."

She got in the car and fastened the seatbelt.

"The car's been good?" he asked.

She nodded. "No problems at all."

"Great. Let me know if it does anything out of order and I'll get it to our family mechanic."

Our family. The words melted her. "Thank you," she said and her voice finally cracked with the emotion she'd been holding in.

He leaned off the door. "We'll talk later."

Raine nodded and pulled off, glad to have him in her rearview mirror as the first tear fell from her eyes.

Chapter 14

Night had fallen on a long day and with it came freezing cold and the threat of bad weather. Raine opened the door. A blast of frigid air filled her foyer, but with it came the warm and welcome figure of Gage Jordan. Here he was again and Raine was ridiculously glad to see him.

Rapid falling sleet framed his silhouette in the moonlit ink blue sky. He looked so good. Like Jesus, Idris Elba and a good macaroni and cheese casserole all rolled into one.

"I guess our date could have been for tonight," he said. "I know I should have called, but I don't know what excuse I would have used for asking to come."

She wanted to say, she didn't care, but she knew that would make her sound, what did the women in the break room at work call a desperate woman? Hungry? No, it was thirsty. And they were right about it. Seeing him left her parched and wanting more every time he left her. Parting from him this morning did absolutely nothing to stop her from thinking about him all day. She stepped aside and let him enter.

"It's freezing," she said of the bone chilling sleet that covered his coat. He pushed the door shut, removed his coat and hung it on the coat rack. "Can I get you some coffee or tea? I think I might have some hot chocolate."

Gage paused like he was considering his choices. She wondered if she was supposed to have brandy or cognac like in the movies. Raine didn't have any alcohol in the house. She didn't drink. She had no idea if he did either. She hoped not. Her experiences with recovering alcoholics at Hope House made alcohol a "no" for her.

"I'll take the coffee," he said. He wiped his boots on the rug.

"You can rest your shoes at the door if you want. It's up to you. I'm not funny about the carpet."

Raine retreated into the kitchen. Her heart was pounding. She needed a second to get her emotions together. When she'd asked him what he wanted to drink, her voice cracked. That was embarrassing. She was always embarrassing herself. Always awkward. That's why they'd teased her in high school and called her "Strange Rain" and "Falling Rain". Some were crueler with names like "Acid Rain". One girl even asked her, "Don't you hate your name? I mean like who ever wants to see rain coming?" She hadn't forgotten that.

Her mother's abrupt placement of her in public school in the tenth grade after having homeschooled her for the other nine years was complete culture shock. She had spent her entire childhood with adults instead of people her own age, so she didn't know how to fit in, how to dress, what to say or even what to think. That not knowing continued into college and even now in the workplace.

She wondered what Gage thought about her? Did he see the oddness or was he such a nice man that it didn't bother him? He was in her house after all. Her heart began thudding again at the mere thought.

Get it together, Raine, she told herself. But her time in which to do so was cut short. No sooner than she'd put a pod in the Keurig, Gage entered the kitchen.

He was bootless. He leaned against the doorjamb and watched her fuss over picking a mug. In the six years she'd owned this house there had never been a man in it that wasn't her father or one of the men from Hope that was handy. It felt so strange to have his masculine aura occupying her space. The faint scent of his cologne permeated the room. Strange, but nice. Raine now realized how so many women got themselves shacked up with men. They added something pleasant to the atmosphere, or at least Gage did.

She decided on tea for herself, filled the kettle with water and put it on a burner. She was glad for something to do with her hands, but when she was done she had to face him. He'd crossed his arms over his chest. Muscles he'd no doubt earned in his military training were bulging everywhere. She struggled to pull her eyes away from his body. She nearly dropped the mug. "Cream?" Her voice was a broken whisper. "Sugar?"

He smiled like he knew she was nervous. Heat filled her face. Ashamed, she turned away.

"A little sugar," he replied, stepping closer. Through her peripheral sight she saw him take in the kitchen décor. "You have a good eye. I noticed that yesterday, but I didn't get a chance to mention it."

Raine had been avoiding looking at him, but now she raised her head to catch his eye. She opened her mouth to thank him. Before she could, he went on.

"I'm practically color blind. That's why I stick with basic solids, army green, army beige, and army brown. That way I don't mess up."

She took a sideways step away from him, sliding the mugs and silverware with her. "Wearing a uniform must have worked out perfectly for you."

"Might have been why I signed up."

She laughed softly and it eased some tension. "I'm sure it was more about duty or something along those lines."

He shook his head. "Not really. I'd finished my degree at UNC and I had no idea what I wanted to do for a living."

"I would think 9-11 would have had you thinking about a job hunt not Uncle Sam's Army."

"I joined in July. I finished boot camp a month after September 11th, so I was already in."

"What made you reenlist?"

"I loved what I did. Plus, when you're trained and in command of troops you care about them. I don't want to sound arrogant, but I started to realize that my leadership could be the difference between life and death in combat. When you're at war it's hard to walk away from that responsibility."

"But you might have if you didn't love your work."

He shrugged. "Maybe."

"Loving what you do." She crossed her arms over her chest. "Such a foreign concept."

Raine lost herself in her thoughts for a brief moment, then she continued. "I was a social work major when I first went to college. I wanted to help people like my parents did. I had an economics class during my second semester and the professor told me he thought I was wasting my talents in social work, that I should consider being an econ major. Numbers and anything related to numbers always came easy for me, so I thought about it, but decided to stick with my first love." She paused. "The summer after that was the first time one of my parents became ill. My dad came down with pneumonia. He was in the hospital for a week. When he came home, I overheard him telling my mother to cut his medicine in half so it would last. They didn't have any money. I mean, I knew we were poor, but I don't know… That was the day I decided I needed a career where I could earn a good salary. My parents were in their seventies. I had to be able to help them, so I changed my major."

Gage nodded. He was right. He was a good listener.

"It was good to be able to care for them. I had been saving for years. The only thing I purchased was this house, because I needed the tax write off, but everything from my handbag to my car was purchased with my savings goal in mind."

"Do you regret those choices?" Gage asked.

"No. But my mother's illness took everything. Cancer is expensive, especially when you don't want to wait for social services programs to approve this and that. I know some people have to, but getting her well couldn't wait. The cancer was spreading fast, so I paid cash. I went through close to a hundred thousand dollars in a few months. Hope House was paid for. I had to borrow some of the equity to pay for her private duty nurse." She was still now, remembering those days not so long ago. It was painful.

She raised her eyes to his and met compassion. "I tried to save her. She wanted to go. She was ready to die. She wanted to be with my dad, but I needed her here with me. I fought against her wishes. I insisted she try different treatments even when she didn't want them. I knew once she was gone that I'd have no one else. I have no family. I don't even have friends really. I'm all alone in the world."

Gage took a few steps closer and raised a hand to stroke the side of her face. "You're not alone, Raine."

She reached up and covered his hand with hers, leaned against it and soaked in its strength and warmth. She tilted her head back. Her mouth parted. *Kiss me*, she thought. She wanted to yell it.

The whistling kettle stole the moment. Gage pulled his hand away and stepped back.

She sighed. She really did have bad luck.

She poured water over her tea bag and put sugar in both their mugs before handing one to Gage. He turned, Raine followed him into the living room and sat next to him on the sofa.

He glanced at her like he was shocked that she hadn't chosen a chair across the room. If he was surprised, he had no idea how she'd surprised herself. It felt natural sitting next to him, but the truth was she'd claimed her favorite seat before she even realized it.

"Do you really think we can save Hope House?" she asked.

"I don't know," he said. "We can try."

"I can't believe you made a decision to do this so quickly," she said. "You seem so cautious. Impulsiveness doesn't strike me as being a part of your nature."

"I've been leading a large battalion for years. Leadership, particularly in a combat zone requires you to make snap second decisions, but you make them based on good information." He took a sip of his coffee and continued. "Hope House kept its doors open for nearly thirty years. Your parents were doing something very right and very necessary. Sometimes all you need is a dream and hard work. You let God do the rest. He'll bless it, if it's in His will."

She took a sip of her tea. "My father said that all the time."

"That's biblical, that God will bless the fruit of our hands."

"Deuteronomy chapter 15 verse 10," she replied.

"Chapter 24, verse 19 and chapter 30 verse 9 and probably about a hundred other scriptures," Gage added.

Impressed, Raine raised an eyebrow. "You know the Bible inside and out."

"I read it on the battlefield for years. It was my comfort."

Her heart smiled. "You're so strong."

Gage had been resting his back against the sofa, but now he sat forward. "You say that like you're comparing my strength to your weakness."

She shook her head. "I am weak, in ways that you'd hate to know about."

Gage chuckled. "Are you trying to convince me not to go into business with you?"

"Probably, because I haven't even convinced myself that I want to do this. Are you sure Hope is what you want?"

"I'm positive," he said. Raine could hear confidence in his voice.

"What if it's too much money? What if the house is a money pit?"

"It passed the code inspection last year. Which makes me wonder how it's condemnable at this point."

"It may have barely passed code last year," she said.

He nodded. "That's possible. But my brothers know structures. If they think the houses are in good shape, they are."

They sat in silence for a few minutes. He finished his coffee and she her tea. Then she stood and took both cups to the kitchen. When she returned, Gage was doing something with his phone. Raine excused herself upstairs to the restroom where she brushed her teeth and hair. She added a little blush to her face and a bit of eyeliner. If he hadn't surprised her, she would have been dressed for him. She'd have taken her sweats off. She wondered if it was too late for that. It would be so obvious, but she decided she didn't care. She was not going to sit in front of him looking like she needed a room at Hope House. She went into her bedroom for a change of clothes.

Chapter 15

Gage's phone had been on silent. He had missed a couple calls from Cade and one from Troy. He returned the call to Cade first.

"Hey, where you at? I've been trying to reach you?"

"I can see that," Gage replied.

"Did you talk to Troy?"

"Not yet. I'm calling you first."

"There's something wrong with the inspection report for Hope."

Gage frowned. "Wrong like what?"

"There are things listed in the report that aren't wrong with the house. I don't know how to say it other than to say it, it's either a big mistake or it's a fake."

"So what do we do?"

Cade chuckled smartly. "It's still we, huh? Okay, *Raine*, because it's her house needs to file an appeal. She also needs to pay the taxes or at least put a down payment on them. I recommend that first."

"Okay."

"You know it has to happen right away. The city is going to take possession by the end of the week. Once she pays the taxes, she can appeal the report."

"That doesn't sound too difficult."

"Talk to Troy. The time to appeal the report has long expired. It's not so easy, but he can explain better than I can."

Gage nodded. "Thanks for calling, man."

"You know we have your back. Keep me informed. Let me know what you need me to do."

"Right," Gage replied and then ended the call. Next he called Troy. He listened to him talk legalese about the situation and then said, "Tell me what we do."

"I'll file the appeal on her behalf in the morning. I have a contact in the city office. A sweet little honey I've been seeing off and on, you know…"

"Troy." Gage cut him off. "I know you got a different woman in every zip code in Charlotte, so spare me the details."

"Don't be a hater, man." Troy cleared his throat. "Anyway, I'll text you when I find out more about the inspectors that did the report."

"What are our chances?"

"I don't know, cuz. All I know is if that report is fabricated, someone has been paid to do it and that someone is going to put up a fight. They'll want those buildings down fast so they don't get found out. I've got to go now, but tell Raine I'll call her first thing in the morning. I need her signature on a few things. The judge will read the appeal request by early afternoon and put it on his calendar quickly. Be on standby for a court date. "

They talked about a few other details and ended the call just as Raine emerged at the bottom of the stairs.

She'd changed into a pair of jeans and a soft looking pink sweater. He noticed she had on a little makeup too. She had made simple changes, but they stirred the man in him.

"I wasn't expecting you." She fussed with her hair. "I didn't feel comfortable."

"You looked great before. You look better now." He smiled cheerfully. She looked better than great. He whispered under his breath, "Down boy."

Raine sat on the coffee table ottoman in front of him. For a woman who was shy she managed to vacillate between being introverted and brazen like she had a split personality disorder.

She smiled at him and looked away shyly. His heart thumped. He could see she was working hard to come out of her shell. He liked that she was trying as much as he liked her. Raine's innocent spirit contrasted so much with all the evil he'd seen in the war. He wanted to possess that spirit in her, but he realized to have it, he would have to have her.

"Tell me more about the military," she asked. She crossed her ankles and dropped back on her hands.

He leaned forward, caught a whiff of her perfume and then decided it was better to resist temptation. He sat back. "Again? You know most of it."

"What was the best part about being in the Army?"

He smiled a little. "Feeling like I was making a difference. Like my service mattered."

"It did," she said sweetly and it did more for his self-esteem than anything anyone had said in months.

She asked him more questions about things he couldn't imagine she cared about, but he answered them anyway.

"You have a curious mind, Raine Still," he said. He reached for a sofa pillow and fingered it because he needed to do something with his hands. He had to stop himself from pulling her to him and finishing the kiss he stopped last night.

She pursed her lips. "I like to know things."

"I can see that. But now what about you? Do I get to ask fifty questions?"

She laughed. "I'm boring."

He moaned a little. "Not possible."

She smiled that small shy smile he'd come to love and looked away. When she turned her head back toward him she asked, "If you think I'm so interesting, why won't you kiss me?"

Chapter 16

He frowned and then she frowned. She realized she'd been too forward. She must sound thirsty.

"I told you why," he replied.

"I don't believe that's it."

"Then what do you think?"

"I think you want Hope House and that's it."

"Raine…"

She raised her voice an octave. "You feel sorry for me. I think you felt sorry for me that night we danced all those years ago. Your mother put you up to it."

He shook his head. Where had this come from? "Nothing could be further from the truth. I danced with you that night because I wanted to. I really wanted to."

Raine turned her head. "Yeah, that's why you wouldn't even give me an address when you left the second time. What soldier doesn't want a letter?"

He shook his head. "I had a lot going on with me at that time. It's not as simple as you think." He paused but then continued his protest. "You are a beautiful woman."

"Then kiss me."

Frustration peppered his tone. "Raine, it's been a really long time since I've been with a woman. I don't want to lose control. I don't want to take it too far."

"But I want you to. I want…" she paused. "I don't want

to die a virgin to everything." She let her eyes slide in his direction. She wanted to see his reaction. Would he be disappointed or worse even, disgusted that she was a virgin?

He sat back like she'd hit him with a pillow. He was surprised, she knew that. But he wasn't disgusted. If he was, he hid it well. "You're thirty-four. Why would you die a virgin?"

She shrugged. "I don't know."

"You do know." He reached for her arms and pulled them to him. Then he raised the sleeve of her sweater to reveal the scars.

"You think we could make love and I not see these?"

"The lights would be out," she replied, smartly.

His eyes become hooded. "I wouldn't make love to you in the dark." He let go of her arms, but their eyes were still locked.

Raine had no idea what the implications of that were, but her stomach flipped and heat rose to her face. She was out of her league. She couldn't out barb him.

He stood like he needed to put some distance between them, stuck his hands in his pockets, and leaned against a wall across the room. "Tell me why you tried to hurt yourself."

Her eyes became moist. "Only if you tell me why you care?"

He shook his head. "Why wouldn't I care? Even if I hadn't gotten to know you over the last day or so, I'm a Christian. I care about people."

She was angry when she spoke. "All Christians don't care about people. It's not some quality that's downloaded after a person gets saved." Bitterness leaked from her pores. Raine knew it was ugly, but she also knew what she was saying was the truth.

"That's true," he affirmed her. "But I think most of us mean well, sometimes our perception and our lack of understanding of what God wants gets in the way."

"It's in a lot of Christians' way." She sighed and closed her eyes to the memories of all the people who were supposed to be Christians that had let her parents down at Hope House. Volunteers who didn't show, partners who didn't provide promised funds or even worse, wrote bad checks that cost them. Even on their death beds, the church was a no show. She'd had to do everything by herself when her mother and father had done so much to help the people in the community and the struggling members of the church.

"The church can't be the reason you've tried to kill yourself."

"Are you here to analyze me? Am I some kind of psych project for you?"

"My psych projects are long behind me. I'm asking because I think maybe if you talk about it…"

"I won't kill myself."

"Right, maybe you won't." he paused. Gage waited, hoping Raine would feel the weight of his concern and then said, "Raine, you are a young, beautiful, smart, woman. I don't understand why you'd do that to yourself?"

"All wars aren't fought in combat, Gage. Some of the hardest fights are for our own lives."

He returned to a chair, but sat across from her. "I'm sorry. You're right." He took her hands in his. "I'm not trying to analyze you. I feel drawn to you. I want to be around you. I want to get to know you, but I have to know what I'm dealing with."

She laughed, but there was no humor in her tone. "What

you're dealing with? Like, am I demon possessed?"

"I know you're not demon possessed."

More dry laughter erupted. "Maybe I'm just crazy."

"Raine…"

"Is that what they teach you in psych? A person who wants to end their life is crazy?"

"Not really and it doesn't matter what I was taught."

She shook her head. "You couldn't possibly understand."

"I've been in a war for nearly fourteen years. I've lost men who were like brothers in that war. I understand a lot."

She was silent now, like she hadn't considered that. As if it made sense. She was quiet for a long time, but then she decided to trust him. "I hate being alone, Gage. It's as simple as that. I want to be with my parents, because they are the only people other than my best friend that I've ever been close to."

"What about your best friend then?"

"She moved to Arizona last year. She got married and she's pretty much gone."

Gage's Adam's apple moved up and down sharply before he spoke. His eyes were empathetic. "So it's the loneliness."

"It's so awful sometimes that I can hear it. It's deafening and defining at the same time," she cried. "It's not that I want to end my life. It's that I don't have a life and I can't stand it anymore. You have no idea how hard it is to have nobody." Tears streamed down her face. He took her in his arms, shushed her and rubbed her back. *God, he felt good.* Raine hadn't felt this good in…she had no idea how long.

"You're not alone anymore," he whispered raising a

hand to wipe her tears. "I want to be with you."

Hearing those words made her want to cry more, but in a different way, for a different reason. She lifted her head. She wanted to look him in the eye when he answered. "What are you talking about? You've spent a few days with me. You could disappear too."

"I'm not going to disappear."

"I don't believe you. You don't know that for sure. No one can guarantee they'll stay."

"If I'm wrong about it, what's the harm in holding on until I do leave? What's the rush to quit on life? I'm here now, so stay with me. Just for a little while and see how this goes." Gage relaxed his hold. Raine pulled out of his arms.

Their eyes were locked in a battle of wills. Gage was winning. He was stronger, or was he just more sure of what he was saying? Raine didn't know. "That's a lot of responsibility for you. My life. My will to live on your shoulders."

Gage smiled a little. "I'm up to the challenge."

"To save me?" Her tone asked the question.

He let out a long exhausted sigh. "Maybe I need someone to save, Raine, and maybe that makes me as desperate as you are." Gage hung his head for a moment, but then looked back up at her. "Besides, I don't believe I'll be saving you. What I think I'm doing is convincing you to take some time to get past this depression."

She smirked at the silly thought that came to her mind. "So, like a probationary period to keep someone alive?"

He chuckled. "What kind of therapist would I be if I couldn't coach someone back to themselves? I mean with one on one attention surely I should be able to change your mind. If not, I need to get in a different business."

She swiped at her eyes and wiped the last of her tears. So much for looking pretty, but he didn't seem to care. "The notion of having you around all the time is tempting."

He smiled. "I love how honest you are. No games. No pretentiousness. Whatever you think comes out of your mouth."

"That's supposed to be a good thing?"

"It's refreshing to know I'm always working with the truth."

"That's so hard for me to believe. You're so handsome and perfect and confident and …"

He ended the barrage of compliments. "I'm just a man and believe me when I tell you, I'm not perfect. I have my faults and I have my demons."

His eyes connected with hers again in that longing way that made her stir inside. He must have felt it too, because he made a noise deep in his throat. It was part groan, part growl. "I should go."

She shook her head. "Please don't. I'll be good." She sounded like a child even to herself.

It was Gage that shook his head this time. His cell phone vibrated in his pocket. He reached for it. It was a weather alert about icing. "That's a sign that I should get on the road before it gets too bad."

Raine smiled at his resistance. "I think it's a sign that you should stay longer." She paused before gathering her nerve. She said, "You can stay overnight."

Gage glared at her with questioning eyes.

"In a separate room. I have three bedrooms."

"Walls don't keep people apart." He shook his head and ran his hand down her arm. "Be glad that I'm strong. It's Christ in me. I'm strong in HIM, and you'll be wanting to see that one day."

"Well, answer me this," she said, standing and stepping closer to him. "Do you find me attractive? I just want to know for future reference."

He chuckled again. "Being this close to you is one of the hardest things I've had to do in a long time."

Raine wrinkled her nose. "If we go into business together won't that be mixing business with pleasure?"

"I don't know." He feigned a confused expression. "You haven't said yes to business yet."

She looked in his eyes and whispered. "Pretend it's a hypothetical question."

"If you want me to say yes to pleasure you're going to have to become my wife."

She didn't think she'd heard him clearly. "Did you say your wife?"

"I took a vow of celibacy a few years ago, Raine. The next woman I make love to is going to be Mrs. Gage Jordan." He stood and looked at his watch before adding, "You say a prayer for me and I'll pray for myself to make it home safely." He walked to the door, put his boots and coat on, waved goodbye, and walked out.

She was completely humiliated. She read books and watched movies. Men did not turn down sex. It was just like her to finally want to give herself to someone and he be strong enough to say no.

He was celibate and she was a virgin. Seemed like the perfect fit, but Raine didn't want to be a virgin anymore. Not now that her stomach was fluttering and every inch of her had been awakened by him. She recounted the many times she'd heard preachers talking about celibacy and clean living and fornication. Never in all the times that she'd heard one of those messages did she think they pertained to her. She didn't have any options. If she had someone to have sex with she'd probably be fornicating. Raine was pure because she simply didn't have choices. She was a virgin by default, not because she wanted to be.

But now Gage had left her curious about the purpose for those who weren't like her. If sex was so great and so plentiful, why would he deny himself? Had she managed to do something that she should actually be proud of?

Raine realized she didn't have the convictions that Gage had. She'd gone to church her entire life, but she didn't have the answers to these questions. She wondered if she could find them in the Bible.

She went into the kitchen, locked the front door along the way and made herself another cup of tea. Then she located her Bible and settled into her favorite chair.

When Raine looked at the full girth of the book, she realized she hadn't really read the Bible very much beyond what was required in church. She stared at the unassuming text and now she wondered, had she been missing something all these years by ignoring it. She closed her eyes and decided she would begin her journey through the book with whatever scripture her finger landed on. She opened the Bible and then opened her eyes. Her finger was in the middle of Isaiah Chapter 40, verse 31. *But those who hope in the Lord will renew their strength. They will soar on wings like eagles; they will run and not grow weary; they will walk and not be faint.*

She read it a few times and by the third time she knew what it really meant. God was speaking to her through her father. Telling her she needed to have hope. She thought about Gage's plea, "Hold on for a little while longer." He practically begged her to not kill herself. Tears filled her eyes and her soul. She decided to pray. She'd already forgotten that she needed to pray for Gage, so she closed her eyes.

The voice of her mother came into her heart, *"Get on your knees, Rainey. God hears you better from a low place."* She had been five years old the first time her mother told her that and she'd prayed on her knees through college. One evening shortly after her college graduation, her mother walked in on her praying. Later, her mother asked why she was on her knees. It was then that they talked and her mother explained that "low" meant from a place of humility, not literally on your knees. The knees were symbolic. She'd asked her mother why she made her get on her knees as a child. *"Because children don't know what it is to be humble. For children the knees are a symbol of humility. When we mature, we put symbols away and meet God with our hearts and spirits."*

But it was too late for change. When Raine really wanted something from God, she got on her knees, so she slid to the floor like an obedient and humble child before Him.

She prayed for Gage first, that he would travel home safely. Then she began to pray about the issues on her heart. Her loneliness, her fear, Hope House. She even prayed about her relationship with Gage, whatever it was, she wanted it to last, even if he remained a friend. She liked him. She liked him a lot and it was not easy for her to like people or at least that was what she'd convinced herself of as she dealt with rejection over the years. She closed the prayer as she had been taught, "In Jesus name. Amen." Raine then pulled her body up and sat on the sofa. She felt better than she'd felt in a long time. And since she was in the space of connecting with God, she decided now would be as good a time as any to read up on the mystery of celibacy.

She swiped her iPad for a browser window and tapped out the words *scriptures about fornication*. There were lots of them in First Corinthians and Timothy. She turned the pages in the Bible until she read all of them. One in particular stuck out in her mind. First Corinthians 6 verse 9. She read it out loud, "Do you not know that wrongdoers will not inherit the kingdom of God? Do not be deceived: Neither the sexually immoral nor idolaters nor adulterers nor men who have sex with men."

She had read this scripture before, but never had it sent such a strong message to her. Now Raine understood why Gage chose to practice celibacy. The word was clear that fornicators would not see God.

Not see God, she thought. Not go to heaven? If she didn't go to heaven, she wouldn't see her parents again. If she didn't go to heaven, she'd be in hell. Was that possible? She'd have to read more of the Bible to understand. Maybe she'd ask Gage to teach her some things.

She stood, stretched and prepared herself for bed. Gage was still on her mind, so she sent him a text message.

I prayed for you. Text me when you get in. Let me know you're okay.

Moments later, she received a message back: *Almost there. Thank you for praying. That means a lot to me.*

She smiled inside. It meant a lot to her to have someone to pray for. She replied: *No texting while driving.*

Fancy phone. Talk text. He answered.

She laughed and then he sent another one: *Forgot to tell you. Troy will call you in the morning.*

She replied: *I'll be ready for him.*

He came back with: *I am really looking forward to our date tomorrow.*

She realized in all their talking tonight that she had not even asked him what his plans were. She shrugged. She needed a surprise. She needed a shock, so maybe it was best that she hadn't. She responded: *Me, too. No more texting until you get home.*

He replied: *I'm pulling in the driveway now.*

She smiled. He was safe. That made her so happy. She knew she was emotional, but losing people had been the story of her life. She replied: *Good night.*

It took a minute, but then he finally came back with: *Sweet dreams, Raine.*

Dreams of you, she thought. She placed her phone on the nightstand and rolled over away from it. She had a date with Gage Jordan. She fell asleep remembering the last time she'd spent time with him.

"Raine."

A handsome male voice hovered above her. She looked up into the face of Gage Jordan and nearly swallowed the hunk of sandwich in her mouth whole. She chewed until she could speak and then took a drink and greeted him back.

"It's been years. How are you?" he asked.

"I'm good." She nodded.

"Do you mind if I join you?"

Raine glanced around the mall food court. It was packed. There was probably no place else for him to sit. "Of course," she replied, moving the empty tray she'd carried her food on over to the seat next to her.

He smiled, put his shopping bags down under the table and sat with excellent posture in the chair across from her. "So, how have you been?"

She sucked in her breath, closed the novel she'd been reading and tucked it into her handbag. "I've been great." She shrugged. "Are you home on leave or have you gotten out?"

"Leave," he replied. "And it's ending in a few days. I'm doing some last minute shopping."

She nodded. "You were deployed the last time I saw you."

"Yeah and I'm going back overseas again. Iraq this time. This is my third tour."

"Wow. I don't know what to even say about that, except, thank you for your service."

Gage chuckled. "That's sufficient," he said before biting into his hamburger.

After he ate a bit he asked, "So, do you live around here?"

She nodded. "I do, but even if I didn't. I love Southpark Mall. It's my favorite place to shop."

"Where do you live?"

"Today, I live over by Sharon Amity and Randolph, but I'm house hunting in the Fort Mill area."

He nodded. "Nice. Good time to buy with the dip in prices."

"Yes," she replied. "I'm not sure I'll buy down there. It's kind of far from my parents, but I'm in love with the affordable new construction."

"New is nice. My father owns a construction business. They are doing a lot of work on that side of town." He smiled and those teeth nearly blinded her. She couldn't help thinking she should have worn some makeup.

He took a few bites of his burger, which amounted to him nearly swallowing it whole, finished his drink in one slurp, and tossed his trash in a nearby receptacle. "So, what kind of shopping you getting into?"

She looked at her Sephora bag and said, "Perfume and makeup. I'm done."

He nodded and then a curious expression came over his face. "What are you doing this afternoon?"

Raine was caught off guard by that question because she couldn't imagine why he wanted to know. "Cleaning my apartment." She shrugged. "Finishing this book."

"Have you seen the new Will Smith movie?" he popped his fingers. "I don't remember the name of it."

"The name escapes me too," she replied. "And no, I haven't."

He looked at his watch. "It starts in fifteen minutes. You want to go see it with me?"

The movies with someone? She was used to going alone. Kiara was a germophobe. Hence, she hated the movie theater and would only go once a year when some popular have to see sister-friend film was released.

She hesitated with her response. Was this a date?

"I didn't offend you by asking you that did I?" Gage asked. He seemed genuinely concerned about it.

"No, of course not. I just…I don't know. You caught me off guard. I guess I'd love to see the movie. Why not today?"

"Cool," he said, sitting back and taking his phone out. "I'm going to go ahead and pay for our tickets, so we can just walk in."

Paying for tickets was definitely a sign that they were on a date. Friends paid their own way. She and Kiara always went dutch. She smiled and stood to throw her half eaten lunch away. She was too excited for food now and besides they had to be at the theater in less than fifteen minutes.

They were in their seats in twenty, enjoyed the movie and then Gage was ready for an early dinner. They ate and laughed. They even browsed a bookstore for a while. When they were done, Raine felt like she'd died and gone to heaven in his company, but then the trip to hell began.

"I had fun. It was cool hanging out with you today," Gage said.

"When are you leaving?"

Gage cracked a little bit of a smile. "In a few days."

"I should write you," she offered.

He hesitated, like he didn't think it was a good idea. "I don't have my address yet."

Raine surmised there had to be a way to contact him, but he offered nothing. Not an email or even for her to contact Brooke, so she let it go. She told herself it wasn't a date. Dates were planned. They had been two lonely people spending time together. She rolled over and picked up her phone. Swiped it and looked at his text message again.

I'm really looking forward to our date tomorrow.

She had been excited about it, but now she wondered why she was getting attention from Gage Jordan. Was he really interested in her or just lonely again?

Chapter 17

Gage ended a call with Troy. He'd talked to the judge briefly and the news about Hope House was bad. They had a court date on Thursday morning. Even though Raine was technically his client, he begged Troy not to call her with the bad news. "Just let it play out the way God wants it to play out," he said to Troy. His cousin granted him that favor. Gage was grateful. He wanted to spend the evening with her without Hope House sitting between them.

At six sharp, Raine opened the door. She already had her coat on and her handbag in hand. "Hi," she said. A smile spread wide across her face.

"Hi back at you," he replied. He took a moment to feast on the gorgeous lines of her face. His eyes lingered over the curve of her lips lined with shimmery lipstick. Gage took in the rest of her. Raine had done as she was instructed and put on a pair of jeans, but she'd not opted for a casual shoe. She was standing tall in a pair of spiked heeled boots.

"Are my shoes going to be okay?" she asked.

Gage smiled. In his opinion, those boots told a lot about her. They were daring and sexy. "Your shoes are perfect," he said, resisting the urge to tell her the effect they had on him.

He helped her into his truck. Once he climbed in, he looked over at her and announced, "I have two ground rules for the evening. One, we are going to have fun and two, no talking about Hope House."

"I can't even ask you if you talked to Troy?"

Afraid his words would give away the truth that he had spoken to Troy, he shook his head no.

Raine raised a hand to salute him. "Yes, sir." She giggled.

"You got jokes." He put the car in drive and pulled out of his parking space. "I am serious and I'm holding you to them."

"Well, where are we going anyway? Blue jeans were not what I had in mind for my first," she paused and then, continued. "Our first date."

He glanced over at her, hoping not to see disappointment on her face. He was rewarded with her near child-like expression. Her eyes were wide with excitement. Her lips were brimming with a smile. No, she wasn't disappointed. Not in the least. Gage turned his attention back to the road and pushed the button for the stereo. Luther Vandross' *Take You Out* strategically filled the car. He danced in his seat to it and looked over at her. She was blushing. He laughed at himself and her and answered the question she'd asked him. "The place is only five minutes away but with traffic, it's going to take us thirty."

His estimate was right on the nose. Thirty minutes later they pulled into the parking lot of a Home Depot Shopping Center. He stole a peek at Raine. Her face was a mask of confused frustration. He smiled inwardly as he pulled his car around a corner and parked in front of Painting With Us. Raine squinted as she looked out the window. He left her to be curious and got out of the truck. He opened the rear lift gate and pulled out a large picnic basket. Then he walked around and helped her out of the truck. She looked at the basket. Gage could feel her excitement. "I was wondering what that smell was. What's in there?"

"My brother Chase is a chef. I have no idea. I just put in my request and picked up the basket."

She rubbed her hands together. "I'm starving and I love

gourmet food. This is the best date ever already," she said turning towards the building.

Gage smiled at her words. *Grateful already*? They hadn't even done anything. He had nowhere to go but up. He closed the door and stepped beside her.

"Is that what we're doing?" Raine asked pointing at the sign.

"We certainly are."

Painting With Us was one of those BYOB, bring your own bottle and make a painting places. He'd asked Cree for an idea and she was quick to suggest it. He trusted his serial dater sister to know what a woman wanted.

Gage pulled the door open. A woman scooted from behind the desk to greet them. "You must be Raine and Gage. Welcome to Painting With Us." She clapped her hands together. I have you set up. She led the way. "You're the only people back here tonight."

They passed a wall of artwork and pictures of people and groups holding the paintings they had done. The place was a nice size, so there had to be more than a hundred pictures.

Gage felt Raine's hand on his arm. She stopped him with words that came across as a plea for help. "Gage, I'm not good at artsy things."

Amused he stopped walking. "Neither am I. I assure you, you won't be alone."

She spun in a circle, taking in the various paintings and pictures and continued, "But I'm really bad."

"It'll be okay." He raised a hand to cup her chin. "Trust me."

The worry lines that had been etched around her eyes and mouth disappeared. "I trust you," she said. She smiled a little as if it pained her to acknowledge so out loud.

He suppressed a smile and removed his hand from her face.

"My name is Mary." Mary's voice interrupted their moment. "You are set up here in our V.I.P. section. I'll take your coats." Gage put the picnic basket down and slid out of his coat. Raine did the same. They handed them to Mary. "Let me know if there's anything I can do to make your time with us more pleasurable. The class should be starting soon." Just as she walked away, the door opened. A group of people entered and Mary went to greet them.

"V.I.P.'s huh? That must have cost a fortune." Raine took a seat.

Gage laughed. He'd never known a woman to care about what he paid for anything. Most women he'd encountered just wanted more. "Gives us a little more privacy," he said. "You'd be surprised at the deals you can make at the last minute. Not like I've had it booked for weeks."

Raine smiled like this pleased her. Then she spun around on her chair. "Okay, Picasso. I don't want to hear a thing if you don't get your money's worth out of me. You're colorblind and I'm visually challenged. At least I can hand you the blue paint. What are you going to do to help me?"

He raised a finger to poke her empty canvas. "I'll help bring out your muse."

"And if I don't have a muse?"

"Good food will make it all better," he replied. "I don't know if you drink, but I don't drink and drive, so I chose not to bring wine."

Raine shook her head. "I don't drink."

"Cool." He pushed the lid of the basket up. "I have

some soft drinks and appetizers for us. I think it's enough to get you full."

He looked down in the basket. His brother had hooked him up royally. He owed Chase big time for this spread.

A few more people entered. Mary returned to them and said, "We're going to start in a few minutes. I'm only expecting one more couple."

Gage looked at his watch. It wasn't seven yet and the class was scheduled to begin then.

"Can I just say, it's an honor to have you here this evening, Captain Jordan. I appreciate your service."

Gage smiled and thanked her for thanking him.

"I hope you and Raine enjoy yourselves. I'd love to get a picture with you when we're done, if that's okay."

Gage nodded. "It would be my pleasure."

"I have cups if you need them," Mary offered. "The restrooms are in the rear. I'll be back to check on you as we move along."

Mary left them and Raine gave him the side eye. "Did we use Veteran's preference to get this spot?"

He laughed from his belly. "There are some perks to serving."

"What did you say to her?"

"Actually, I didn't say a thing. Her husband took my call. When I told him my name, he recognized it. He's a vet himself."

"And you're a celebrity," Raine teased.

"If that gets me V.I.P. access, I'll take it."

He stood and excused himself to the restroom. He washed his hands and came back to an empty area. He looked around and found Raine walking and looking at the different pictures towards the front of the studio. Instead of joining her, he took a seat and observed her. She studied the canvases and while she did, he studied her. She was nervous about this, but still, she was taking a chance and doing it. She could have said, "No, this is not my idea of fun," and insisted he take her home, but she hadn't. Maybe she was stronger than even she knew. Maybe Raine Still just needed an opportunity to explore things and live her life.

Mary was wearing a headset with a microphone. She went to the front of the room and asked everyone to take their seats. Raine rejoined him. "This looks hard," she said. "But I think it'll be fun, right?"

His heart filled just hearing her say that.

Raine gave Mary her full attention and Gage watched her from the side. It baffled him how this beautiful woman was not only single, but had managed to move through life without losing her virginity. He'd be lying to himself if he didn't admit that seemed appealing. Not because he wanted an untouched woman, but because he wanted to date a woman his age and he didn't want her to be carrying a luggage set full of relational baggage. Most women he met were so messed over by no good men that they waited for him to mess up too.

Raine turned to him and clapped her hands with excitement. "Alright Picasso," she said removing a bottle of paint from the workstation. "It's time to paint our midnight blue skies."

Chapter 18

Raine stood back while Gage took pictures with Mary's husband. She had been in six shots herself. They'd done a group shot that included the entire class, a couple's shot, a shot with Mary and then a shot with Mary and her husband. She was starting to feel like a celebrity and she was just Gage's date. How awesome it was for people to admire him for his work and dedication. She hadn't even realized the gravity of her position with him. She was the woman who was with Gage Jordan and he was a war hero. Raine had still been thinking of him as the captain of the football team. He was so much more than that.

They laid their masterpieces in the back of his truck and took the short ride to her house. Raine lay back against the headrest and let the words of Alicia Keys song, *No One* penetrate her emotions. He had good taste in music. Gage reached for her hand. She opened her eyes and looked over at him. He took his eyes off the road for a second and smiled. She raised his hand to hers and kissed him on the back of his. Then she closed her eyes and reclined her head again. Raine reveled in the magic of this moment. She thought about how days ago she was actually contemplating ending her life, seriously thinking about it again and here her life had changed in a matter of days.

They pulled in front of her house. With regret, Raine sighed over the fact that the night was coming to an end.

"Can I ask you something really personal?" Gage's voice spoke over the music. She turned to face him just as he was turning the knob to reduce the sound.

145

"Of course," she replied.

"What do you want? If you could have anything happen in your life right now, what would you want?"

You, she thought, but she knew she couldn't say that. So she thought about what "he" represented and she realized it was love and family. Love because she was already falling hard for him and if she could have him, she would have a husband and a lover and beautiful brown babies. Family because he was a Jordan and being with him would mean she would instantly have sisters and brothers. Family is what they represented. She wanted both, but she couldn't say "you", so she said, "A family."

"You mean, like a husband and kids?"

"Yes," she replied, "and in my case, in-laws and nieces and nephews."

Gage turned his lip up and nodded his head like he was deciphering scientific data.

"I know it sounds old fashioned," she added.

"No, it doesn't. Why would you think that?"

She shrugged. "The women I work with are so career driven which I don't think is bad, but they talk like wanting a family is some kind of Puritan ideal. I was glad I started teleworking. The conversations about money and disposable relationships got old."

"I think more women want that than you think. They just don't want to be slaves to it. You know, with husbands that expect them to do everything."

She raised an eyebrow. "Are you old fashioned like that?"

"You mean wanting a family or being a dinosaur with my woman?"

She laughed. "Both."

"My mom was a stay at home mother for many years, but my dad always helped her with the house. He cooked and cleaned and helped with homework and laundry. Not a lot, because he worked long hours for a long time, but every day he did something to remind her that he was in this with her even if it was just to bathe us and get us into bed so she could sit down. So, my lady, I learned that marriage is a partnership. Raising a family is a partnership."

"That's nice."

"That's why Nathaniel and Evelyn Jordan are happily married. Emphasis on happy. He honored my mother and she honored him."

"That's why they keep having anniversaries."

He smiled and she could tell he was thinking about them. "Yeah."

"And the second part of the question," she began. "Do you want that?"

He grimaced before answering. "Yeah, why wouldn't I?"

She didn't think her question was so silly and she let him know with her tone. "Because you're still single and you've never been married right? I can't imagine that it was hard to find someone who wanted to marry you."

"If you think a good man is hard to find I can tell you a good woman is equally as difficult." Gage avoided her eyes by playing with his car keys. "Besides, I didn't think it was the right time before. Being deployed is hard."

She challenged his response. "Soldiers get married all the time."

He looked at her. "Maybe I say that to make myself feel better about being an odd duck because you're right, most of the men I served with were married or in serious relationships."

"So," she prodded.

"I guess the truth is if I had met the right woman when I was serving, I would have begged her to take that ride with me."

Begged. That word sounded so intoxicating coming out of his mouth. She couldn't resist asking, "What does the right woman look like, Gage?"

He hesitated for a long time, but never pulled his eyes away from hers. "She looks a lot like you."

Raine's stomach did a somersault. She never in a million years thought he'd respond with that answer. Her lips parted and then she closed them again. She didn't know what to say.

"I'm going to kiss you now." His tone was authoritative, but gentle, just like him.

Her stomach flipped again.

"I'm not kissing you because I'm caught up in the moment. I'm kissing you, because I can't fight it anymore." He leaned toward her. His hand slid upwards. Paused at the pulse in her neck. Fingered her jawbone. His lips were close enough for her to feel the heat of them.

"You never start anything you're not going to finish," she said, raising her hands to his face. She wasn't letting him get away this time. She met him the rest of the way.

His lips were warm, but sweet and gentle, almost tentative. Heat rushed through her body, her stomach fluttered like it held a hundred butterflies and her heart...her heart felt like it would burst. The kiss was long, exploratory and explosive and it had probably gone on much too long. Raine realized she'd never stop and maybe Gage sensed that as well, because he was the one who pulled back.

He released a long breath, rested his forehead against

hers and spoke her name. "Raine." She closed her eyes, breathed him in, and waited for him to speak. "I'm falling in love with you."

A heart could stop and the person survive. She knew that for sure, because it had just happened to her.

Chapter 19

Gage entered his parent's house. The smell of baked goods filled his nostrils. His father was at a church board meeting. It was no surprise that his mother was baking. Whenever his father had a board meeting at the church, she rewarded him with a decadent dessert. Her treat for the pain and suffering he swore he endured keeping a civil tongue with the stubborn group he served with. Gage had called ahead as not to startle her. He let his nose follow the scent to the kitchen. His mother was taking a pan out of the oven. It was a pecan and caramel something that looked like it contained enough sugar to put his overweight father in a diabetic coma.

Gage removed his jacket and hung it on one of the hooks in the mudroom. He kissed his mom on the cheek before sliding onto a stool at the island. She placed the tray on a cooling rack in front of him.

"What in the world is this ridiculously sinful looking delicacy?"

"Pecan Cheesecake Squares. Your father loves them."

Gage cocked an eyebrow. "No doubt about that, but I thought he was trying to lose twenty pounds."

"Your father isn't trying to do anything. He's lost four pounds since Christmas but only because I'm substituting healthier ingredients in his meals. I have found that if I make him something really delicious from time to time, he cuts back on the junk he picks up on the road when he's working. Or at least that's what your brothers tell me."

She removed her oven mitts, leaned against the island and drank him in with her eyes. A smile tipped her lips. "So, what are you doing on this side of town at ten at night on a weeknight?"

Gage chuckled. "Weeknight. Mom, I'm not in school. I don't even have a job to go, so the weeknight thing…"

She shrugged. "You're here for something."

He nodded. "My mother's advice."

Excitement filled her tone. "Good. I like giving my children solicited advice. It makes me feel like I'm winning."

He chuckled again. "Okay, so this should really boost your ego. I need advice about a woman."

Now it was his mother whose eyebrows furrowed. "I need to sit down for this." She pushed herself onto the stool next to him and waited for him to begin.

"I'm falling in love with Raine."

His mother appeared to be surprised. "Falling in love?"

"Yes, in love. I mean, I may already be in love. Is that crazy?"

"You may be your father's son." She smiled.

Gage wanted to believe that too, but he couldn't help second guessing himself. Raine was lonely. Maybe he was too. "I feel like it has to be wrong."

"Tell me why you think it has to be wrong?"

"It's too soon for one thing and I don't know. I don't even know what I want to do with my life. Not really."

"You have the interview next week."

"For a job I'm not going to take," he said and his answer was definitive. His decision was made.

"I'd say knowing what you don't want to do is a good

start." His mother shook her head and stood again. She went to the stove, removed the kettle and added water to it and returned it to the burner.

"You know being a mother of seven children had its challenges. There's never enough money and there certainly isn't enough time. The one thing I tried to do was allow you each to be your own individual person. That's why there were no group punishments and no group parties. I so enjoyed seeing the uniqueness in each one of you. Seven different little people came from my body and that was such a gift from God." She smiled warmly. "Now that you're adults, I enjoy it even the more."

Gage held his tongue. He had no idea what this had to do with his problem, but he waited.

"Do you remember a boy from your childhood, Tommy Westerfield?"

Gage squinted. "From like twenty-five years ago? The one who shot his cousin with his father's gun."

His mother nodded. "Nearly thirty years ago. You were seven."

"Vaguely."

"The Westerfields hadn't been in the neighborhood long. Tommy and Chase became friends. Chase loved being around that child, so one afternoon I invited them inside for a snack just so I could talk to the little boy and get to know him. They ate cookies and drank milk and went back outside." She placed a hand on her hip. "You probably don't remember what you said about him."

Gage shook his head and chuckled again. "No."

"You said, 'He has a dark cloud on him, Mommy.'"

Gage sighed before speaking. "That sounds like me. Always finding the dark clouds."

His mother moved closer to him and took his hands in hers and squeezed. "No, my son, that's your gift...discernment and sometimes the clouds are dark. They're dark before the storms." Gage was stunned into silence by her words. She continued, "I didn't let your brother go to his house after that, because what you said shook me. I felt strongly that you saw something that I had missed and then…"

"He shot his cousin."

"The police never believed it was an accident, but they had no proof."

Gage shrugged. "Maybe they were villainizing another black male."

"Possibly." She smiled. "But I couldn't help feeling like you had warned me about a dangerous situation. You saw a spirit on that poor child. And then you continued to do that over and over and over again throughout your childhood. I could count on your gift to help me see what I couldn't see."

"What are you saying, mom?"

"Trust your instincts. You have good ones." She raised a hand to her chest and beat it once. "Trust your heart. It's filled with the Spirit of God and He will never lead you wrong."

Kissing Raine had made him feel complete, but he felt like he owed his mother more of the story. "Raine is different."

"Yes," his mother nodded. "Raine had a very different upbringing, so she's a different kind of woman, but if you find that attractive and interesting, don't let what you think *should* be get in the way."

"That's not what I mean, mom. She's not in a good place emotionally, maybe not even mentally."

"And you're thinking she needs to be whole for you to be with her?"

"I'm thinking that's what I should be thinking."

"You're a therapist. You were a therapist before you decided to go to school to become one." His mother chuckled. "I don't know what's going on with her, but you may be over analyzing. Every half needs another part."

Gage felt his eyes get moist. He'd just been thinking how Raine made him feel complete and here his mother was repeatedly using the word half. He had his confirmation, but still, he shook his head and admitted his truth. "I left part of myself in that desert. I feel responsible for J.J.'s death and I'm not over that. I don't know that I ever will be, so maybe the person I'm really concerned about is me."

"Maybe what you both need is love. It covers a multitude of faults, son." His mother took his hand in hers. "Sometimes all a person needs is someone to care about them and want to be around them. Look at Brooke. She was in a bad place before Marcus found her."

Gage nodded, remembering how depressed Brooke had been when her husband began having an affair with her best friend and then married the woman after Brooke divorced him. He'd never liked Andre, but now Brooke was engaged to a man Gage himself approved of.

"Anyway, you were away for that year with Brooke. She spiraled into a terrible depression, but Marcus didn't care. He loved my daughter to life. If I never knew the power of love before, I witnessed it then. So help her, son. Help her live a little. Your gut is telling you she's worth it or we wouldn't be having this conversation."

"Maybe we'll help each other," he said. His mother smiled at him. He stood, wrapped his arms around her and squeezed tight. Squeezed as much of her love out of her as he could get before he released her with a kiss on the cheek.

"That's what I came here for."

She patted his hand. The kettle whistled just as the garage door rose signaling his father's arrival. His mother turned off the burner and poured three mugs of water. "You don't have school tomorrow, so have some sugar with us."

Gage smiled. He couldn't think of anything he wanted to do more.

Chapter 20

Raine spun her chair around and reached for the paper that her printer had just spit out. The receipt for the tax bill for Hope House. She let out a long breath and placed it on her desk. She felt relieved. Who had she been kidding? She couldn't live with herself if she let it go. But then she had to admit the truth to herself. She hadn't been planning to live and she figured if she was going to kill herself, why put up a fight.

Everyone wanted to know why she hadn't been fighting for Hope House because they didn't know her deep dark secret.

She looked across the room at the table near the window. The pills she'd been counting and the letter she'd been writing. How had she let herself get back there again? She had no right to end her own life. She'd learned that in her Bible reading last night. Suicide was self-murder and murder was wrong. God would never want her to do that. God did not want her to give up. She had her entire life in front of her. She had a future.

"I'm trying too hard," she whispered, thinking of how she was trying to convince herself of this fact. She knew her renewed enthusiasm for life had more to do with Gage Jordan than the words she'd read, but still...maybe God was using Gage to help her hold on until she was stronger.

"Stay with me. Just for a little while and see how this goes."

She closed her eyes to his words and melted inside. He knew just what to say.

Raine stood and walked over to the table. She picked up the pills and the letter. Before she changed her mind, she walked back to her desk and shoved the letter in the paper shredder. Her heart was thudding so loudly that it drowned out the sound of the shredder, but still, she saw it disappear. Then she looked at the bottle. Two months of sleeping pills. Enough to make sure she never woke up. She left the room with them, entered the kitchen, and stood in front of the trash can. She removed the lid and poured the pills into her hand. Her entire arm trembled with the weight of them. Not the weight in grams, but the weight of their power. Had she really been planning to take all of those pills? Her eyes misted over when she answered her own question. "Yes, I was going to do it. I was going to kill myself." Raine turned her hand over and dropped the pills in the trash. Then the bottle. She removed the liner from the can and pulled the tie to close it. Intent on getting them out of her house, she went out the garage door.

The biting winter wind cut through her body all the way to the bone, but she continued her walk to the curb. Tears streamed down her face as she reentered the house. Raine let the garage door down, fell back against a wall just inside the house and slid to her knees with relief.

"I'm falling in love with you."

Life could change for the better in an instant.

***

Raine and Gage were summoned to Troy's office to discuss the legal action against Hope. If the size of his office was any indication of how well Troy was doing with the firm, he was more of a success then he'd given him credit for.

"We're not quitting on this, Troy." Gage's tone was

firm.

"I'm not quitting either. I filed the paperwork to request an appeal."

"How long will it take for the hearing?" Raine asked.

"It's tomorrow. That's why you're here. But let me be clear, the hearing is for the judge to determine if he'll allow the appeal."

"Tomorrow," Raine replied, releasing a long sigh. "That's so soon."

"The city takes possession on Friday, so you know this is an emergency action with the court," Troy stated.

"So, you're saying this is a request to request an appeal?" Raine was confused. "I thought everyone could appeal."

Troy looked at her pointedly. "You had the right to one. That right expired four months ago when the initial report was filed on the condition of Hope. Did you get any letters?"

Raine nodded. Ashamed, she looked at Gage as if he was asking the questions instead of Troy. "I don't even know if I opened all of them. After my mother died, I was too depressed to care what the city had to say."

Gage patted her closed fist reassuringly.

Troy continued. "It's okay. I'm just asking so I have the facts correct. If you didn't get letters that would help our case."

"Does she stand a chance of getting the appeal?" Gage asked.

"I'm not going to pretty it up for you. It's not going to be easy, but we'll try. It helps that Hope has been in the community for so long and with such a good record of being a well-run organization."

Raine nodded.

Troy stood. "I'm not a pessimist. I like to win especially when it's family, but I'm telling you to be prepared for the worst, because the worst could definitely happen."

Raine nodded to indicate she understood and forced herself to appear optimistic. "Thank you for helping me out. I appreciate everything you've done."

She and Gage stood and Troy walked them to his office door and then to the elevator. He shook Gage's hand and gave her a friendly pat on the arm. "Try not to worry too much," he said before he disappeared down the hall back to his office.

Raine sighed loudly. "I really messed this up."

Gage turned her body toward him. "Baby, don't be so hard on yourself. It's not over yet."

Baby. She loved the sound of that, but it didn't take away her guilt. "It sounds over."

"The judge will grant the appeal. The community –," Gage stopped mid-sentence. The elevator opened and they got in. But even after the car started again, Gage's face still held a curious expression.

"The community what?" Raine asked, prompting him to finish his statement.

"I've got an idea," Gage said and he looked like some kind of light bulb had gone off in his head.

"What is it?" she pressed.

"Just let me see if I can pull it together," he walked her to her car, and waited for her to get in and start it. "I'll call you later."

"Gage," Raine pleaded. "Tell me."

"I need you to trust me. I don't want to get your hopes or even my own hopes up without doing some legwork."

She frowned. She hated secrets. She was a big baby about them. But then she looked into his dreamy brown eyes and realized she'd deny him nothing, so the word "okay" slipped easily from her mouth.

Raine watched him walk - if that swagger of his could be called that - to his truck and climb in. She still couldn't believe that she was in a relationship with Gage. A relationship that was more than a friendship. Friends did not kiss like that man kissed her last night. Friends did not say: *"I'm falling in love with you."*

She had no idea where this was going, but she knew it was moving in the right direction. She just hoped Gage Jordan didn't hand her heart back to her. He was falling, but she was already on the ground.

Chapter 21

Raine changed into her pajamas and climbed into bed. She was exhausted. After she returned from Troy's office, she spent most of the evening catching up on work she needed to have done for her crazy boss. She considered the implications of tomorrow's ruling. If she got to keep Hope House, she'd have to quit her job to run the place. Maybe not immediately, but once the building repairs were made it would need to be staffed and occupied. She had no idea where to begin to find people. She had to have a competent person to run the place overnight. They would be sleeping on site. Then she had to find a few volunteers to help with managing the operations. Her parents were there all the time. They lived there, but she didn't want to live up on North Tryon. Not by herself.

Once again, all the questions she'd had when she'd decided not to keep Hope were coming back to her in a flood. Raine refused to let them overwhelm and depress her, so she reached for her Bible. It had become her constant companion. She closed her eyes, said a prayer and opened it to Isaiah. Isaiah was her father's favorite book. She was quickly making it through the book and planned to get on some kind of Bible in a year reading schedule when she finished it, but for now it gave her comfort to read the scriptures that her father had committed to memory.

She came to Isaiah 43 and read the text. Then she went back to verse two and repeated it:

When you pass through the waters, I will be with you; and when you pass through the rivers, they will not sweep over you. When you walk through the fire, you will not be burned; the flames will not set you ablaze.

"God, it's like you're inside my head," she whispered. "How do you know just the right scripture to give me when I need it?" Raine wondered at that for a moment, but then instead of questioning it, she read the scripture again, this time out loud. "When you pass through the water, I will be with you; when you pass through the rivers, they will not sweep over you. When you walk through the fire, you will not be burned. The flames will not set you ablaze."

Raine closed her eyes again. This is what she needed to know. That she was not alone in this. That God would carry her through all the difficulties she might encounter with Hope House. He was telling her loud and clear. This problem would not overtake her. She would not get hurt.

"Thank you, Lord." She whispered the words from the depth of her heart and placed the Bible on her bedside table before turning off the lamp and nuzzling under the comforter. She closed her eyes and prayed some more. Specifically asking the Lord to tell her what to say tomorrow and to show her if there was anything else she could do. "Show me if I'm missing something, Father," she whispered into the quiet of the room.

She pulled the comforter tighter around her shoulders and prepared to doze off in what she thought would be minutes. But it didn't happen. She was tired, but her mind was still alert. She couldn't stop thinking. Raine looked toward her closet door. She should have figured out what she was going to wear in the morning, especially since she planned to leave her house before seven in order to make it to the courthouse by eight-thirty. She was not going to make herself get out of her warm bed, but she mentally went through her wardrobe. She tended to hibernate in the winter, so her selection of court appropriate clothing was lean. She had several early fall suits that might work, but she wasn't even sure how cold it would be. Especially since this winter had been uncharacteristically cold. She reached for her phone and pressed the weather app. It spun and spun but didn't open. Raine groaned and reached for the remote control. For some reason, she had to know what she was facing and she wanted to know before she fell asleep. She clicked the remote and switched the channel to the ten o'clock news and sat up. Raine didn't watch the news very often. It was all bad or at least they tried to present it that way. She preferred to get her updates from the local paper and a few blogs she followed. No negative visual stimulation. She learned that from her father.

"Reading bad news as opposed to seeing it doesn't leave the same tattoo on your soul," he'd say as he sifted through the morning newspaper. She smiled thinking about his words.

She turned up the volume and watched a few local stories. One was about a small store owner who was fighting the county. They were taking his land through the eminent domain process to expand a local school. Raine felt his pain, even more so than her own, because there wasn't anything wrong with his business and it was being taken from him.

"That's so unfair," she whispered to herself and then she got an idea. She gasped audibly. How could she have not thought of this sooner? She muted the television, threw the comforter off her body and leapt out of bed. She crossed the room for her iPad. Sleep would have to come later.

Chapter 22

Under the cover of a large umbrella to protect her from her namesake, Raine walked up the steps of the courthouse. Gage met her at the door. Ever the gentleman, he was holding it open for her.

Nathaniel Jordan and another inspector they'd hired were coming also. If permitted, they would testify that the city's report was inaccurate. But even with that, Troy said the odds the judge would overturn his own judgment were rare. A private contractors word didn't weigh as much as those employed by the city. Besides, the judge's position was that Raine had ample time to contest the city's report and she hadn't. The shame of that weighed heavily on her heart, but at the end of the day, she realized that she couldn't go back in time and fix it. All she could do was try to make things right. That was what she was doing now.

They entered the main lobby. Raine smiled and waved when she caught the eye of Gage's father.

"You look like him you know," she whispered, observing him from the distance. He and Cade were in what appeared to be an intense conversation with a man Raine assumed was the other contractor they'd hired.

"I pray I'll always be half the man," Gage replied.

Raine squeezed his hand. "You're more than half."

He smiled back and said, "Let's go on in. Court begins in a few minutes."

Raine cleared her throat and looked down at her watch.

"We have a few minutes. Let's wait here."

Gage frowned and said, "I'd really like to go in. I have a surprise for—,"

"Gage Jordan!"

Raine smiled as she spotted her own surprise flying through the lobby.

It was a reporter from WCNC News and her cameraman. A man and another cameraman with the emblem for Fox News on it followed them.

"Right on time," Raine said.

Gage looked at her curiously.

"Mr. Jordan and Ms. Still. Do you care to share with the viewers for WCNC why you're here today?"

A satisfied smile crept over Gage's face. "Give us thirty seconds," he said to the reporter and then he swept her a few feet away. "You called the media?" he asked, incredulously. "How did you get them to care?"

She twisted her mouth into a smart smile. "Well, your fame comes with some power. I told them you were planning to work with veterans at Hope and they were all over the story."

Gage shook his head. She could see admiration in his eyes. "You're amazing. You know that? Amazing."

She let out a satisfied breath before saying, "Let's go talk to them before they find a bigger story."

He agreed and they turned back to the reporters.

"Are you ready now?" The female reporter asked.

"We are," Gage stated.

She and the male reported cued their cameramen and then said, "I'm here with Gage Jordan. You'll remember

Gage Jordan. The Vice President pinned the Silver Star on him just last month for his distinguished military service."

She continued to run down his resume and then when she put the microphone in front of Gage, he told the story that the entire city of Charlotte was sure to empathize with.

Raine was proud of him. She didn't think she could be any more impressed with him. That is until she walked into the courtroom. Her mouth gaped open.

Seated in a small cheering section just behind the plaintiff's table were Mrs. Belk and a group of three homeless men that Raine recognized as veterans, including the young man Gage had just given money to on Sunday. She could feel the tears coming. She was going to cry ugly. She reached into her handbag for tissues. She'd bought plenty in anticipation of the moment of victory or defeat, but now it mattered even more. She wished she'd known she would be this emotional. She'd have bought the entire box of Kleenex.

"I guess we both had the same idea," Gage said.

Raine swiped the first tears from under her eyes. "Great minds think alike."

Gage pointed his finger heavenward. "The Lord's purpose prevails."

"That's in the Bible, right?" she asked.

He smiled. "Absolutely. I'll show you where later."

They slid into seats next to their guest. Raine wrapped her arms around Mrs. Belk. "Thank you so much for coming."

Mrs. Belk squeezed her hand. "Baby, I wouldn't have missed riding in that fancy Hummer for anything in the world. Plus, you know I believe in what you're doing. I'm so proud of you. Your parents would be proud."

Raine smiled under the blessing of her kind words, and then she shook hands with the three men and thanked them for coming. All three were somewhat teary eyed and that saddened her. In their eyes, she saw all that was riding on this judgment; the futures of the people who needed Hope and her future as the person who wanted to give it to them. She felt horrible for how she'd let time get away from her. She only hoped she had a chance to make it all up and do the right thing. Raine closed her eyes and said a silent prayer for Jesus to fix it and make it right, even in the midst of all that she'd let go wrong.

When she opened her eyes, she found Gage's eyes on her. "It's going to be okay," he said. She hid her shame behind a weak smile and let out a cleansing breath.

The bailiff called the court to order and instructed them to rise for the judge. Before the judged entered, the reporters came into the courtroom with their cameras.

The judge swept into the room and sat. It was pretty obvious the reporters disturbed him because he frowned before whispering a message to the bailiff. The bailiff stepped out of the courtroom, taking the reporters and their cameramen with him. A few minutes later, the reporters came back in and took a seat as the bailiff went back to the judge's bench and whispered to him.

Gage leaned in and said, "Now the judge knows about the media angle."

She agreed it looked that way.

The bailiff called the court calendar, which included five other cases. The judge reordered the cases to accommodate meeting with them first. The justification being that he wanted the reporters to leave before the other cases began to afford the other plaintiffs privacy.

Troy had them come to the plaintiff table. A tiny spitfire of a woman in an expensive, fashionable and form fitting suit flew into the courtroom and pushed the swinging partition open. She dropped her attaché case and coat onto the defendant's table.

Troy smiled and approached her. "Ms. Monroe, I was thinking you were going to miss another opportunity to lose to me."

The woman turned, crossed her arms over chest and said. "Since when do you need the media to help you with a judgment?"

Troy shook his head. "Their being here is a surprise to me."

The judge banged his gavel, silencing the low murmur of noise in the room. "Attorney Monroe, we appreciate you joining us. If you're ready, I'd like to hear this case."

Raine was impressed with Troy. He used a lot of words that went over her head, the main one being *In Rem Remedy*, which she figured out, was an action the City Council would take against a property that they deemed needed repair or demolishing. The city had done everything in order from the initial filing of the paperwork to the appeal. Troy's position was that the report of the repairs was not accurate, which in turn did not give Raine the information she needed to make a decision about the property."

Attorney Monroe's position was that Raine had an opportunity to appeal and did not do so, therefore had no right to ask for an appeal at this point. Attorney Monroe was finishing her statement when the judge interrupted.

"I've made my decision on this case," he barked.

Troy popped to his feet. "Your Honor, if I could request testimony from some members of the community about the importance of this facility."

The Judge looked down his glasses at the little group of people Gage had gathered and then he looked past Raine to

Gage. "I said I've made my decision, counselor, now please be seated." Troy and Attorney Monroe sized each other up and took their seats. The judge began.

"I have found that the Plaintiff, Raine Still, has been negligent in her efforts to keep the property. The building has been vacant, in disrepair and in general a nuisance to the community as evidenced by multiple police reports citing vandalism, disturbance of the peace and a recent response from the fire department.

However, I do think the variance in violations cited by the city and those identified by the witnesses for the plaintiff should give the court pause. It is never the intent to add the burden of demolition cost to a private citizen who is attempting to make repairs."

Attorney Monroe groaned audibly and Troy smiled.

"I have also considered the good that would be if Hope House were to remain in the community, particularly if Mr. Gage Jordan will offer his counseling services to our homeless veteran population. So, for that reason, I am granting the appeal. I order the city to complete another inspection. If an *In Rem* Action is required at that time, another date will be added to the calendar to address such." The judge paused, removed his glasses and looked directly at her and Gage. "Ms. Still and Mr. Jordan, Godspeed in reopening Hope House. We thank you for your distinguished service, Mr. Jordan and appreciate your desire to continue to serve your fellow man." He banged the gavel and yelled, "Next case!"

Raine jumped to her feet and threw her arms around Gage. He picked her up off her feet and whispered, "I knew it, baby. I knew God would come through."

The bailiff asked that they move along so the next group could take their places. Once in the lobby Raine hugged them all: Gage's father and brother, Troy, the vets from

Hope and Mrs. Belk. She couldn't stop crying, but she knew she needed to say something. She hated that she had to do so in front of the news cameras, but then she considered the business side of it all.

"I want to thank each and every one of you for your help today. My parents were good people. They spent their lives giving and taking care of other people and that includes me, an abandoned baby in a hospital waiting room that they gave a home to. I lost sight of the importance of their work, until I was reminded of how much Hope House meant not only them, but to the community as well."

The reporter from WCNC pushed the microphone in Gage's face and asked, "Were you satisfied with the judge's ruling, Mr. Jordan?"

Gage cleared his throat. "Of course we were. We now have an opportunity to make the necessary repairs and reopen the facility."

"How do you intend to pay for the repairs?" The male reporter from Fox asked.

"We'll begin some fundraising immediately. If you'll share the address for Hope House with your viewers, I'm sure the people of Charlotte would be willing to assist us with our work."

They badgered them with a few more questions and then told their crews they were done.

The rest of the group dispersed as well. Gage's father and brother said their goodbyes and left to go to job sites. Troy and Attorney Monroe seemed to be locked in an out of court battle that Raine suspected was fueled more by their obvious attraction to each other than the law.

"Well now," Gage said getting her full attention. "It's just you and me."

"I can't think of anyone I'd rather be alone with," she

replied, reaching for his hands and then she got serious about what she was going to say next. "Thank you for helping me, Gage. Thank you for helping me get to this place." Tears began to flow down her cheeks again. "So much has happened since Saturday, so much in my heart, my spirit and in my mind. You helped me find myself. I feel like I owe you my life."

"You don't owe me your life, Raine. I just reminded you that your hope was in God."

"That He has plans for me. That I have a hope and a future," she said, quoting words from the Bible. "Jeremiah 29 verse 11. I learned that this morning."

Gage smiled. "You have no idea how happy it makes me to know that you are reading the Bible and learning scriptures. The woman in my life has to have a personal relationship with God."

"The woman in your life," Raine teased. "Are you kind of sort of trying to tell me something?"

Gage frowned. "No, definitely not."

Now it was Raine who frowned. Had she misread him? He'd said he was falling in love with her.

"Definitely not, kind of sort of. I'm definitely telling you for sure that you aren't getting rid of me, Raine Still."

She smiled now. "I don't think I want to."

"Good, 'cause you know I know how to show up unannounced."

"They call that stalking," she teased.

"I call it getting my way." He put his arm around her waist and gently led her through the corridor and out the door.

"I have to take the people from Hope back to the neighborhood, but I owe you a night out. Can we meet at seven? We need to celebrate and this time my lady, you can get dressed up."

"Your lady," Raine blushed. "You're spoiling me with these terms of endearment."

"I plan to spoil you with more than that." Gage took a step closer to her. When he did, the air left her lungs. "That is, if you feel the same way about me that I feel about you."

Her eyes locked with his. She thought he should know the answer to that question from looking into her soul. "I can count on you to finish what you start?"

"You can count on me period, babe."

She hesitated for a moment then spoke the truth he deserved to hear. "Then I'm falling in love with you too."

He smiled. Those brilliant teeth nearly blinded her before he lowered his head and sealed their promise with a kiss.

Epilogue

Friday…

Raine couldn't decide on salmon or steak. It didn't make much difference to her. She'd prepared both so many times that she could practically do it in her sleep. She settled on steak, because she'd had salmon last week.

She moved through the supermarket picking up a few other items on her shopping list and then rolled the cart to the register like she did every Friday night.

"Hello, Ms. Still," Amanda, said greeting her.

"Hi, Amanda." Raine was smiling today. Her smile seemed to be contagious, because Amanda who hadn't been smiling was now showing her teeth.

"You must have had a good day." Saying so seemed to please Amanda.

Raine knew she was beaming. "I did. I have to say, I cannot complain." Raine paused putting a few items on the belt. "How about you? Has it been busy today?"

"Yes. It's been busy all week. Cold weather makes people want to shop for food. Bread, milk, cookies, and ice cream. You can tell by the ingredients they're buying that soup is on the menu too."

Raine emptied her cart. "Well, no soup for me tonight."

"Of course not," Amanda said, confirming she knew the Friday night routine. "You have a few extra items though, and I don't think I've ever seen you buy a steak that big."

173

"I'm a hungry carnivore." Gage's voice came in from behind Raine and so did his not so subtle brush against her body. "Is this the one you wanted, babe?" He was holding the can of diced tomatoes she'd sent him to find.

Raine glanced at the can and then over her shoulder at him. "Perfect."

"Like you," Gage teased.

Raine blushed, but then she realized she wasn't the only one embarrassed by his affectionate words. Amanda's face had turned beet red, but she managed to speak. "Paper or plastic?"

"Paper," Raine and Gage sang the word together. Raine thought it was the sweetest chorus she'd ever heard.

Life was good.

The End

Have you read the first story about the Jordan family?

Brooke Jordan thought her Christmas was going to be boring, particularly since she's stuck working in Montego Bay, Jamaica instead of home in Charlotte, North Carolina with her family. Paradise isn't paradise when you're not where you want to be, but this Christmas is anything but uneventful. Three airplanes land on the island and Brooke quickly finds herself in exchanges that cause love, temptation, and HATE to surface. Will she allow an enemy from the past to keep her from giving a little love to the man who wants to be her Christmas present?

Love A Little, Cree Jordan's story - Summer 2016.

About the Author

Even as she pursued degrees in Textile Technology, Organizational Leadership and finally, Adult Education, **_Rhonda McKnight_**'s love for books and desire to write stories was always in the back of her mind and in the forefront of her heart. Rhonda loves reading and writing stories that touch the heart of women through complex plots and interesting characters in crisis. She writes from the comfort of her Atlanta home with black tea, Lays potato chips and chocolate on hand. At her feet sits a snappy mixed breed toy dog. She can be reached at her website at www.rhondamcknight and on social media at www.facebook.com/booksbyrhonda and www.twitter.com/rhondamcknight and www.blackchristianreads.com where she has joined with nine other Christian fiction authors to introduce her stories to the world.

Books by Rhonda McKnight

Breaking All The Rules

-Book One – *Second Chances* Series-

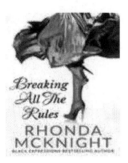

Deniece Malcolm is shocked and heartbroken when she finds out her baby sister, Janette, is marrying Terrance Wright, because she was the one who was supposed to marry him! Everybody knows there's a rule about dating exes. Janette is pregnant and not only is this wedding happening, but Deniece has to arrange the festivities.

Deniece's feelings and pride are hurt, but surprisingly, Terrance's younger, sexier, cousin, Ethan Wright, is there to provide a listening ear and a strong bicep to cry on. Ethan's interested in Deniece, but she has a rule about dating younger men. Despite her resistance, things heat up between them and Deniece begins to wonder if it's time to break a few rules of her own.

Unbreak My Heart

-Book Two – *Second Chances* Series-

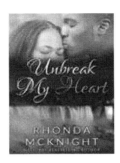

Cameron Scott's reality television show is spiraling into an abyss. When her estranged husband, Jacob Gray, reappears offering a lifeline she realizes she still loves him. Cameron has kept a painful secret that continues to be at the root of the unspoken words between them. Regaining trust requires telling all and healing old wounds that she believes would destroy any chance for happiness they could have.

Jacob Gray left his wife Cameron because she was pregnant and there was no way the baby could be his. Five years have passed and he still loves her, but can he forgive?

An *Inconvenient* Friend

August 2010

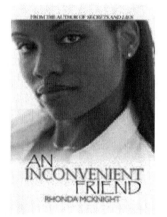

Samaria Jacobs has her sights set on Gregory Preston. A successful surgeon, he has just the bankroll she needs to keep her in the lifestyle that her credit card debt has helped her grow accustomed to. Samaria joins New Mercies Christian Church to get close to Gregory's wife. If she gets to know Angelina Preston, she can become like her in more than just looks, and really work her way into Greg's heart.

Angelina Preston's life is filled with a successful career and busy ministry work, but something's just not right with her marriage. Late nights, early meetings, lipstick- and perfume-stained shirts have her suspicious that Greg is doing a little more operating than she'd like. But does she have the strength to confront the only man she's ever loved and risk losing him to the other woman? Just when Samaria thinks she's got it all figured out, she finds herself drawn to Angelina's kindness. Will she be able to carry out her plan after she finds herself yearning for the one thing she's never had . . . the friendship of a woman?

What Kind of Fool

Feb 2012

The Wife, Her Husband. Their faith. . . . Will it save them before it's too late, or will an enemy from their past destroy their marriage forever?

Angelina Preston tunes out the voice of God when she decides to divorce her husband, Greg. She's forgiven him for his affair, but she won't forget, even though her heart is telling her to. Shortly after she files divorce papers, she finds out her non-profit organization is being investigated by the IRS for money laundering. In the midst of the very public scandal, Angelina becomes ill. Through financial and physical trials, she learns that faith and forgiveness may really be the cure for all that ails her, but can she forgive the people who hurt her most?

Sexy, successful Dr. Gregory Preston didn't appreciate his wife when he had her. His affair with a devious man-stealer has him put out of his home and put off with women who continue to throw themselves at him. Greg wants his wife back, but he'll have to do some fancy operating to get her. When the secrets and lies from his past continue to mess up his future, Greg finds himself looking to the God he abandoned long ago for a miracle only faith can provide.

Samaria Jacobs finally has the one thing she's always wanted: a man with money. The fact that she's in love with him is a bonus, but even so, life is anything but blissful. She's paying for her past sins in ways she never imagined and living in fear that the secret she's keeping will separate them forever.

31503879R00116

Made in the USA
Middletown, DE
02 May 2016